STRANGE ADVENTURES OF A MODEL RAILWAY

By

MICHAEL E. HOCKINGS

ISBN-13: 978-1533296689
ISBN-10: 1533296685

Dedicated to my family and work colleagues who inspired me to write this without knowing.

CONTENTS

CHAPTER 1

The Model Takes Shape

Thomas Pigglewick was in many ways a very fortunate little individual. He was the proud owner of a model railway that many a small boy of his age would be very envious to possess.

The layout had begun six years before Thomas was even born, when Michael, his father, started to purchase items of track in a piecemeal fashion during his lunch breaks from work. Gradually, enough lengths of track were obtained for a complete circuit. Next to follow was a model engine, a black 0-6-0 Class E2 tank of the Southern Railway, together with a green coach. By obtaining a transformer in the same year the system was complete.

For several evenings Michael used to amuse Thomas's elder sister, Marie (Thomas was still not born yet), at bedtime by assembling the assorted pieces of track to form a circuit around the bed of the previous house in which the family had lived. It took quite a while to put everything together, and this did not leave much time for running the trains before having to dismantle it all again and put it all away. Michael's wife, Sylvia, knew nothing of this, and even thought that there were rats loose! Over a period of time more items of railway stock were acquired, starting with more railway carriages of the southern region, and a 0-6-0 Pannier tank of the Great Western Railway. Later on, another Southern Railway locomotive was purchased: this one being an M7 4-4-0 tank engine in black, and two carriages in the chocolate brown and cream livery of the Great Western Railway.

A few years later the family moved to another house in the same district, which had more bedrooms, and a converted loft. Michael decided to start building a model railway for Thomas's third birthday, knowing that it would become a long-term project. The location chosen to base the model on was that of Bridcup in the County of Gaggleshire, because it was a joint Great Western and a Southern Railway with a lot of siding accommodation to take plenty of wagons and carriages. The station had closed to all traffic thirty years before and nothing remained to indicate that a railway existed at all.

Michael did a great deal of research into the station area, using the many books in his collection and his own memory. He hoped to develop a plan matching the original, the area of sidings being nearest to the door to the loft. Late one night Michael lined up the pieces of track on the living room floor after Thomas had gone to bed. A couple of points were bought from a local toyshop, to enable a passing loop to be laid in the Great Western side of the station, representing the real life situation. It was soon realised that some compromises would have to be reached regarding the length of the station platforms, in order to fit onto a piece of chipboard four feet long by two feet wide. This was overcome to some extent by using two lengths of chipboard placed end on, in order to lengthen the platforms. The Southern Region side of the station was also constructed at a later date, using more points especially bought for the purpose, and laying in a connection between the two systems.

After a lot of hard work Michael completed the station area on the two pieces of chipboard, and the station area now consisted of three platforms: the original Great Western platform, a Southern Railway platform, and between the two an island platform, which was shared by both railway companies, as in real life. On occasions Michael worked late into the night on the project, painting the platform surfaces with grey emulsion to simulate tarmac, and gluing brick paper on the platform edges. A packet of model ballast was bought and Michael studied the best way to achieve a life-like appearance to the track. After much endeavour Michael finished the station area, but without buildings, in time for Thomas's third birthday on 20th November.

Thomas was pleased with the result, and played with it on several occasions when it was balanced on an armchair in the living room, although there was only room for one piece of chipboard at a time. Thomas used his existing model engines on the track and buses on the station approach road, even though these were not of the correct scale. The pet hamster enjoyed itself on the layout as well.

Michael later came to the decision to make a portable layout for Thomas using the existing station, as a Christmas present. To do this more tracks would have to be added in order to make a complete layout around a bed. To do this, it was necessary to purchase more chipboard of the same size, but cutting it in half in order to save space and money, and then the track was secured on this, using the flexible type of track because it was cheaper. Michael thought that the best place to do this was in the loft of the house since there was already a lock on the door that he could use to hide the work as it progressed, away from prying eyes. In fact, the loft became sort of a secret workshop for a time with all the tools lying around and mess everywhere. The fact was that Michael wanted the work to remain as a complete surprise for Thomas on Christmas Day, and this was duly achieved, as he knew nothing about it when the day came.

In addition to the layout, a bridge was built over the tracks, being comprised of two separate pieces, and also a tunnel and an engine shed. The tunnel was designed to fit on any length of single track and was called the "1995 Go-anywhere Christmas tunnel". The last two items proved to be very popular with the pet hamster when let out of its cage to exercise!

It was not until well after Christmas that Thomas wanted to use his model. The excitement of having so many other presents meant that Thomas was kept very busy in other directions. Lack of space to assemble the model meant that the railway was left to one side for a few weeks. It was not until the festivities were over, and all the decorations were put away, that Thomas's attention was focused on the large number of chipboard panels complete with track, that were neatly stacked in a corner of the dining room. At this point, Thomas needed help to put everything together, and a decision was reached whereby the only room that would take all the boards was his parents' bedroom. In fact, the model was designed to fit around the double bed, provided that it was moved away from the wall and more towards the middle of the room. It soon became apparent that plenty of time would be needed to get everything in place before train operations could take place. What took longer was that for each of the individual boards, connecting pieces of track had to go in place, and this was a little tricky sometimes as the rail connectors were difficult to line up correctly. The model worked well enough that day, except for a couple of things that needed to be sorted out straight away. For one thing one of the curves was too sharp and the engine kept coming off around one corner. It took a while for Michael to work out what was causing the problem, but he soon set to work in rectifying it. The track had to be lifted up and then re-laid again with a gentler curve, and this solved the problem. However, there was one other defect with the system that would not go away. As the engines went around the track, the connections between them opened up a little every time that the trains went over them. This eventually led to the track separating completely, and the boards moved apart, causing derailments.

Luckily, this happened towards the end of the session when it was time to put everything away again, which was usually after tea one day during the weekend.

*

Thomas liked the model railway, but found it was a bit of a chore getting all the boards from the loft where they were stored in an area set aside for them. For a start it took quite a time to even get the boards down from the loft, there being so many of them. He was only a little lad after all, and his legs ached walking up and down the wooden stairs, and that was before the boards were even assembled. Of course, his father Michael helped out, and he told Thomas he could only play with the model when he had time to help him. It was also important to supervise the operation of the trains, to prevent any damage. The model worked satisfactorily, but it was the time involved to get it all organised. With this in mind, Michael and Thomas agreed the best solution would be a move towards a permanent layout that could be used on any occasion without having to worry about being short of time. This happened after trying out a newly acquired Great Western tank engine on a short length of track. The only place really suitable was the unconverted part of the loft, although it had many disadvantages, namely it being cold in the winter and very hot in the summer, meaning that there would be restrictions on what time of year could be used for all the construction work.

That was not the only problem. There was not

even a floor in this part of the loft. The year before, Marie had put her foot through the floor when trying to hide away from her parents, and made a hole in the ceiling in the bedroom below. Since the family was not insured for accidental damage, they had to pay for the repairs themselves. As a result of this Michael put a lock on the door to prevent the same thing happening again, and had put a floor in that part of the loft, which made it a lot easier to move about in there. It would become essential to extend the floor all the way along this part of the loft before any real work on the railway could begin.

A start on this was made before Thomas's fourth birthday as part of his present, and it made accessibility to the loft easier, as there were other things stored that were required from time to time.

Installing the floor in the loft took Michael a long time, and it was not very rewarding since it made no difference to the model railway, although Thomas could still use it in the same way as he did before. It was not very spacious in the area where the model was going to be installed, and the loft was in complete darkness. There were no lights to use, only a lamp on an extension lead. The joists were uneven, and this made the floor uneven as well. Eventually enough flooring was laid to begin the staging on which the model was going to be built. The staging consisted of uprights screwed into the new floor by brackets and secured into the roof battens. Horizontal members at right angles made the whole thing rigid, and finally, shorter horizontal pieces of battens were nailed into the longer horizontal supports.

The construction of the model railway began in

earnest when the two original sheets of chipboard that made up Bridcup Station were permanently fixed onto the staging. This was a more difficult process than it first appeared, since it meant that four lengths of track had to be connected properly all at the same time (this was one of the things that made the portable layout difficult to put together. In fact not all the tracks were coupled up at this time to make things easier). At this point more baseboards of the original model were sacrificed to provide material to lengthen the station area, and so the portable idea was abandoned from now on. The layout of the original model was now altered so that the Great Western Railway curved in the opposite direction as before, to enable it to fit in with the shape of the loft. More staging was erected at the north end of the loft, and then along the wall in which the entrance door was situated. On this was laid more track. This meant that the layout was now U-shaped, and a terminal platform was constructed just long enough to accommodate one carriage, so trains ran from one station to another and back again. Work was halted on the Southern Railway, except for a steep incline out of Bridcup Station, which was called "Spire Hill". Michael now decided to stop work on the model railway for a time as it was summer and too hot to work in the loft.

*

It was quite a while before work resumed on the railway, since Michael lost a lot of enthusiasm for it due to working in such a confined space. However, it seemed a shame to leave things as they were, so eventually a new start was made. It was decided to extend tracks in a southerly direction from the station, but before that could be done more flooring had to be laid in a third area of the loft. This proved to be a frustrating job because of the confined working space, and the fact that there were overhead beams in place supporting the roof. Another annoying hindrance was that a large iron girder made access even more difficult. Despite all these concerns the floor was duly laid and also all the remaining baseboards to complete the circuit. Enough tracks were then laid to finish the Great Western Railway model, except for a fairly short gap. There then followed another spell of inactivity, during which little happened on the railway until Thomas was over seven years of age, when Michael connected the two ends of the tracks. The system then was complete. Thomas's older sister Alison was present at this operation and the opening ceremony that followed it.

However, the model was not performing well at this stage and Michael decided to put more effort into the task of completing the whole model. One of the engines had a burnt-out motor after a rubber tyre had come off and jammed the wheels. The model was left in a model shop to be repaired, and a family friend called Mr. Perkins telephoned one Sunday night with the estimate. He then suggested that Michael dealt with him direct to save money, so all the other engines were serviced after he paid a visit to the house one night. He had a look at the railway and thought that all that the steel track ought to be replaced with the nickel-plated sort, so that the trains would work better. This would involve relaying about a quarter of the railway, including the last piece that was installed, much to Michael's annoyance.

In the meantime, following a "planning meeting" with Michael, Thomas, and Alison, it was decided that the Southern Railway would be finished that summer, even though that meant a lot of effort would have to be put in. Work commenced on the "Southerly extension", which would be at a higher level than the Great Western track in order for it to clear some supporting roof members. The track-bed was constructed to a much gentler curve and gradient to make it as realistic as possible from the entrance door. To make things a lot easier Mr. Perkins installed lighting in the loft and Michael also installed a plug socket. These two things combined made a big difference in carrying on with the model railway, as up to now Michael had largely been working in the dark.

Work continued apace in extending the Southern Railway in a circuit around to the site of the Great Western halt, which was the temporary terminus at one time. This meant making a bridge over the Great Western, which was called "Spire Hill" in order for the southern tracks to be nearest to the loft door. The track-bed was made up of thin plywood, salvaged after alterations to the garage adjoining the house. The wood was painted black to make it more like a real railway. At this point building ceased and construction re-commenced north of Bridcup Station and over "Spire Hill", after which it curved sharply to run parallel with the Great Western railway on a higher level. On reaching the highest point, the Southern Railway was then built on a gentle descent to gain the same level. The model railway was now open, and three trains could now run at the same time after a double controller was purchased. All that remained to do now was to make the model as realistic as possible by using any scrap material that was suitable for the job. The embankments, when they were first made, were very rough, so polystyrene was packed under the wooden supports, and plaster applied over the top. When dried and painted with different shades of green and brown the whole railway took on a much more pleasing and realistic appearance.

On visits to the town of Tonknose and also Linemouth Guildhall, Michael bought some second-hand buildings for the railway. These included houses and hotels, as well as smaller buildings such as platelayers' huts and small offices. Another lucky buy was a box of small people, and all these items represented a considerable saving on the normal price when bought new.

One of the last jobs that remained was the background scenery and the sky. For this, several sheets of hardboard were purchased from the local DIY shop, although it was very difficult to secure it to the roof members for reasons of accessibility, and being able to support it at the same time as nailing. Michael wished he had done this particular job before the railway construction started, as it would have been a lot easier to reach the awkward areas.

Nevertheless, the model railway was now largely completed, except for the final touches of scenery, routine maintenance, and any further alterations if they were required.

*

Thomas was quite an imaginative boy, and when he slept he often dreamed, although as most people he could not remember by the following morning what the actual dream was all about. One day, however, this was different. It had been snowing all day, which was unusual for the far west, at least along the southwest coast. The whole area around the family's home was covered in a thick white blanket of snow and everyone was confined indoors. The children made a snowman in the back garden, and later in the day Thomas played with the model railway.

Sylvia put Thomas to bed early that night, but he took a long time to doze off. The whiteness of the snow shining through the window made it seem earlier than it was. Meanwhile, strange things were beginning to happen upstairs in the loft. Thomas had left the electricity switched on as he often did, and this in the past had always annoyed Michael. While the family slept, a high wind sprang up and this dislodged the television aerial, making it come into contact with the tracks near Gordon's bridge. This in turn made one of the engines start up of its own accord, which happened to be the original engine or "Black Thomas", as it was known. The engine knocked a box on to the floor that contained the second-hand model figures that Michael had bought in the Guildhall several months previously. The surprising thing was that some of them started to move about by themselves.

Thomas was awakened by the noise in the loft, although the other members of the family still slept soundly. He got out of bed and crept quietly up the stairs to the loft so as to not wake anyone, and opened the small door to the model railway. This time, instead of finding himself in the railway room he felt himself falling down and down in what seemed to him a swirling white mist, and quickly lost consciousness.

*

It was at this point that something strange was happening to the Pigglewick family, who possessed two family pets – a dog called Brutus and a cat named Mandy. Brutus was not allowed in the family home during the night and was forced to reside in a large kennel in the back yard, and even then he was kept on a long chain. Mandy, on the other hand, was given free range and was permitted to go anywhere she wanted to go. One particular night it was extremely cold and the night was clear. This could only mean one thing as far as the two family pets were concerned, and the weather forecast that night was not very good. Heavy snow was predicted which was unusual for the far west. It was unfortunate that both Mandy and Brutus were locked out of the house and left to fend for themselves. To obtain shelter from the bitter cold wind that was becoming progressively worse on that night, Mandy decided to throw caution to the wind, so to speak, and to bed for the night with Brutus in his kennel. This may have seemed a strange thing to do, but Mandy knew she was safe as the two animals got on well together.

However, the two animals on this occasion got on too well together, for just after a couple of months later, a litter of youngsters arrived on the scene which looked nothing like their parents. As they developed they exhibited characteristics of both cat and dog, and so Mandy and Brutus called their offspring kittendogs which became very intelligent over a period of time and assumed an upright posture by walking on their back legs.

Mandy and Brutus decided to give their offspring names that resembled those of the Pigglewick family. The names duly assigned were Mickel and Sylvate after their carers, together with Mareekoid, The Alisose, and finally Tonkas after their children.

The Pigglewick family were rather dysfunctional and never worked as a cohesive unit at any one time, each family member wishing to do their own thing, both Thomas and Marie not expressing their feelings very much to their parents. It was for that reason Mandy and Brutus named their kittendog offspring in a similar fashion to their owners.

CHAPTER 2

In the Bleak Midwinter

Thomas awoke with a shudder to find himself in unfamiliar surroundings. It was dark and cold and it seemed to him he was in an old-fashioned railway carriage; the sort he had been in on preserved railways that his father had taken him to several times before. Thomas was huddled in a corner by the window, and outside he could just about see through the darkness a railway station canopy, under which was a mound of snow. He then looked around him and saw that that the carriage was occupied by three other people who were all asleep, and that they were all strangers to him. Thomas looked to the seat opposite. In the centre was a man that seemed to look similar to his

Uncle David, but he seemed very much younger, and so he discounted this idea. Some of the other people looked like scaled-up versions of the tiny models bought in the Guildhall, as far as he could tell.

Thomas thought to himself, *This is a nightmare, it just can't be true.*

Just then, his foot came into contact with something on the floor. It was a newspaper. As he stooped to pick it up, he noticed the date on the front page. It said 29th December 1962. Thomas was understandably very surprised that a newspaper that old could still exist after all these years, but it was even more strange that it was in such good condition. A cold shiver ran down his spine as he picked up the paper and glanced around him at the same time. In the old-fashioned railway carriage there indeed appeared to be a younger version of his uncle! It couldn't be! Thomas realised that he had gone back nearly forty years in time!

Thomas folded the newspaper carefully and concealed it in a deep inside pocket of his coat. As he did so, a tall man wearing a guard's uniform opened the sliding door of the carriage and shook the shoulder of the person next him.

The guard then said, 'Wake up. You can't stay here all night. The train is stranded in the station because the points are frozen, and it won't be until the morning that we will be able to get them working again. It would be much better to take shelter in the signal box overnight. It's far too cold in here!'

He spoke in such a loud voice that it woke the other passengers, although it took a while to alert them. They all noticed Thomas huddled up in the corner with his arms tightly folded around his waist, and spoke together with surprise and astonishment, almost as a chorus.

'Where did you come from?' They all pointed at Thomas, making him squirm in the corner of his seat.

'I don't remember you getting on this train.'

Thomas tried to find the courage to reply, but could only manage a mumble. 'I… I… I… I moved up from the next compartment as I was on my own and was very scared,' he said with little conviction in his voice.

The other passengers continued to stare at Thomas, making him even more frightened of his predicament, but at that point the guard came to the rescue.

'Well it doesn't matter for now; we will have to sort this out later on. What matters now is that we all get warmed up and find somewhere more comfortable to stay overnight. Like I said, the signalman has offered for us to stay in the signal box until the morning. We will decide what to do when it gets light.'

With that, the man nearest the guard struggled to get up, and the other passengers followed with a few moans and groans as they were all stiff with sitting too long in one position.

The man opposite Thomas gently patted his hand on Thomas's knee, and spoke with a hushed voice, 'Hello young man, I am called David. You look rather like my younger brother called Michael, but he will be tucked up in bed at home, and so should you. I certainly don't know how you got here, but for the time being you had better come with us.'

The guard led the way out of the train and along the snow-covered platform to the signal box. On the way Thomas tried to make out exactly where he was, although this was difficult as it was snowing heavily, and the strong wind blew the snow in his face. He could make out that the train they just got out of consisted of a single engine, something like one of his models, but he couldn't make out the wheels since they were below the level of the platform. The engine itself was green, or at least most of it was. A large proportion of it was covered in snow. As the group passed, it was observed what remained of the fire in the engine was glowing in the dark, and the guard remarked that the fire would have to die down by itself, as it would prove useless to get the engine going again.

David took Thomas's hand, held it tightly, and steered him away from the edge of the platform towards the relative safety of the station building. As he did so he said to him, 'You know you look just like my younger brother when he was your age, and you behave like him as well.' Thomas didn't know whether this was a compliment or not but really wanted to find out where he actually was, and more importantly how to get back to his own time. If he managed to get here in the first place, there must be a way to get back again, somehow.

Before long, the group reached the steps to the signal box, the guard still leading the way, followed by Thomas and David. The other two passengers were now some distance behind and the guard called to them to catch up. As they reached the door of the building it opened as though by itself. This was not the case of course; it was just the fact that a stiff breeze blew through the window. An elderly man in dark blue overalls greeted them.

'Hello,' he said. 'I am Henry the engine driver and this is George the signalman, who has kindly decided to let us stay for the night.' George beckoned everyone to come in, and then closed the door behind them.

When they were all inside it was quite noticeable that it was very much warmer. A fire was glowing in the hearth, and there seemed to be just enough room for them to be able to sleep on the floor. By now the other two passengers had caught up and they in turn were admitted to the signal box.

'So good of you to join us,' said the guard.

What he didn't know was that the taller of the two men slipped in the snow and had twisted his foot, and that the other man was giving some support. At last these two men had something to say; they had been very quiet up to now.

'I can't help if my foot is hurting. By the way, let me introduce ourselves. I am Ivor and this is my friend Bernard.'

Ivor was tall and rather gaunt. As he took off his cap he exposed an almost bald head with a large birthmark above his left ear. By comparison Bernard was shorter and a little plump, wearing a dark, checked sports coat that stood out against Ivor's pale raincoat.

With the introductions over, agreement was made concerning the sleeping arrangements for the night. The signalman had the first say as it was his workplace, and expressed a wish to make himself comfortable in an old armchair near his desk. As he looked round, Thomas could make out a diagram of the track layout encased in a glass-fronted frame. He saw that the station was called Fackleton and that there was only one platform, a passing loop, and a short siding at the north end of the platform which was opposite to the direction from which they had come. At both ends of the station were points, and as it later transpired it was these that had frozen solid. Being an observant boy for his age, Thomas had memorised all this information in one quick glance at the diagram. He was relieved that at last there was a name for the location, although it meant nothing to him at the time. He was also not too dismayed at being separated from his family, as this was nothing new to him. On several occasions in the past Thomas had got lost when the family went out on day trips, and yet everything seemed to resolve itself in the end. What worried him was how to get out of this particular predicament, and also to explain his presence to the other people. He hoped against hope that they would not press him again on this matter.

Just then, Thomas's attention was distracted as the door of the signal box opened once more, and in the midst of a downfall of snow another man stumbled inside and collapsed on the floor. Finding the energy to get up, he brushed the snow off his clothes and still panting, he said, 'What a night! It's no use, I can't get any help.'

He tried to say something else but had to stop to recover his breath, and the guard rushed over to him and sat him down in the vacant armchair. The guard then interrupted the man, and removing his cap, introduced the stranger as Bertram the fireman who had earlier gone for assistance further down the line.

'By the way,' the guard said, 'I don't think that I have mentioned my own name yet. I am called Headeroonie Bill, and I am sorry if I have seemed abrupt, but I am a worried man at the moment. After the railway is closed it is more than likely I shall be out of a job. I am also concerned that my wife is wondering where I am. I should have been home hours ago, as should the rest of us, I dare say.' The adults in the group nodded in agreement.

With the last comment Thomas's mind set to work again. He remembered his father talking about the disused railway that ran through some woods on the outskirts of Linemouth where Thomas lived. If this was the case, he was not too far from home. It was just the time factor that he was concerned about. Perhaps if he stuck with the group of people, somehow he could get back to 1999, the year he left behind. He also remembered that his model railway was based on the area just north of Travelstild up to Church on the Hill, further up on the moors. Fackleton was further south situated in a wooded valley. Thomas also realised that he had better invent a plausible reason for being in the train.

As he was thinking this over, the talking stopped and Headeroonie Bill, the guard, looked at Thomas and said, '…And what do we do with *him?*'

Thomas thought to himself, *I don't like you very much*, as the dreaded question was asked once more.

'Well where *did* you appear from? I don't remember seeing *your* ticket.'

Thomas replied that he was playing "Hide and

Seek" with the other members of the family, and had hidden in a wooden crate. Somehow he fell asleep and someone had put a lid on the crate. It then ended up on the train with him inside. 'That's better,' replied Headeroonie Bill, staring at Thomas as though he was acting as an interrogator. 'I can remember putting a crate on at Travelstild.'

Thomas realised his mistake too late. He had given them the impression he lived in Travelstild and not Linemouth and so had got himself in more trouble, although at least the guard now appeared to believe his story.

'Yes,' continued Headeroonie Bill, 'I thought the top of the crate was loose. I meant to go back and nail the lid back on more securely, but I must have forgotten, what with everything else going on tonight.'

With that, Thomas gave a little sigh and thought to himself, *Thank goodness you did forget to nail the lid back, on or my latest excuse wouldn't hold water.*

The guard then turned around to the others and informed everyone that every attempt would be made to rescue the stranded passengers the next day, and that there would be no more stops until the train reached Linemouth. After that, the branch line would be officially closed. They were to be the last ever passengers on this stretch of track, although arrangements would have to be made to get Thomas back to his parents in Travelstild.

Nothing could be done to contact them in the meantime as the telephone line had been cut north of Fackleton. However, people at Linemouth knew of their plight and a relief train would arrive in Fackleton.

Again Thomas gave a little inward sigh, and another plan was beginning to take shape in his mind. In fact, he remembered his father saying he should have a plan of what to do for every day of his life. 'Having something to do will give you more motivation and make you a well-balanced person,' he remembered him saying. This advice had now proved to be very useful.

'In the absence of the stationmaster who is indisposed, I am taking charge of the situation,' said the guard. 'It is better if members of staff remain here in the signal box, and the passengers sleep overnight in the storeroom below. It means going outside and down the steps, but it will be better for all of us. I have procured enough blankets and other bedding material to keep all of us warm. I will assist you to get safely settled in for the night, and then I will return up here. I cannot allow members of the public near the signal levers in case of any mishaps, and besides, there are too many of us in here.'

Thomas thought (and perhaps the others did as well) that Headeroonie Bill, the guard, was acting in a most pompous manner, but they had no choice but to follow his instructions. Thomas went back to consider his plan for the next day.

I must get away from the others when we reach Linemouth, otherwise they will send me back to Travelstild. Mind you, that might not matter if I am not in my right time anyway. I could be stuck in 1962 and not 1999. Perhaps all this is just a dream, but it seems very realistic if it is.

With that thought, David took Thomas's hand again, and they all followed the guard out of the door, into the cold night air. Ivor shuffled along as best he could with his twisted foot but managed to reach the platform without any mishap.

The guard took a key from his pocket, undid the padlock and opened the door to the signal box, which took a great deal of effort. With a heave the door gradually opened, exposing a gloomy interior. Luckily the light still worked when the guard fumbled for the switch, and the group filed inside. Headeroonie Bill then pointed to the bedding, which was neatly arranged for them, which looked quite comfortable, much to their surprise. Ivor, David, and Bernard thanked Headeroonie Bill for his efforts, and the guard bade goodnight before leaving the storeroom and returning upstairs to the other staff.

The intrepid passengers decided who should sleep where for the night, and then there was a case of lights out. One by one they all drifted off to sleep rather quickly. It had been a long day for all of them.

*

Thomas awoke the next morning wondering where he was. He was afraid to look around him and kept his head under the bedclothes, afraid of what he might see. He went over the events of the previous day in his own mind, and then realised that the newspaper he had hidden under his coat was now beside him. So it was true after all! All that had happened was not part of a dream. He did not want to try and read the paper in the confined space of the bed as he wanted to keep the fact that he had the paper a secret. Instead Thomas summoned up enough courage to peer out above the level of the bedclothes to confirm what he had experienced the day before. Yes, the same people were still there as well, reinforcing the fact that this was reality. Was he never going to return to his parents and sisters? If he were to remain in this time, how was he going to explain his existence, and where was he going to live?

Just then, the door of the room creaked open and Headeroonie Bill, the guard, entered. Thomas screwed up his eyes as the light went on, and the guard closed the door behind him, moving slowly into the room, before stopping at the first makeshift bed. Headeroonie Bill then shook the bedclothes, and it was Ivor who turned his head and opened his eyes.

'Wake up,' said the guard gently. 'It's not quite so cold today. The stationmaster is getting breakfast, and he has invited you all to his house to have something to eat. If you get ready, I will take you there. I've cleared a way through.'

With that, the others started to wake up as they heard that food was mentioned. It was a long time since they had eaten.

Eventually, still bleary-eyed, they all emerged from the storeroom into the daylight, and led by Headeroonie Bill, the group trudged out of the station, along a short path to the stationmaster's house. At the door the stationmaster and his wife greeted them, and they introduced themselves as Richard and Roberta.

'Yes,' said the stationmaster, 'we are known as the two R's in the village.' Thomas thought this was quite amusing, reminding him of his primary school days. 'Do come inside and make yourselves comfortable, breakfast won't be long, but I am afraid it will be quite a while before another train will be able to get through.

Rest assured all that can be done, is being done.'

With that, the group, led by Ivor, whose foot appeared to be much better, went inside; except for Headeroonie Bill, who made his excuses, saying that he had already eaten and that he had a lot of work to do. The conversation was rather muted around the meal table, as Roberta went to and from the kitchen in performing her duties as cook and waitress. However, Richard was most surprised that Thomas was travelling on the railway. 'How old are you?' he inquired, to which Thomas replied, 'Seven,' automatically thinking of his true age back home.

'Perhaps after you have finished your meal you would like to have a good wash; I expect you could do with a clean-up. Then perhaps we can play some games,' continued Richard. Ivor, Bernard, and David thought this was a very good idea, and thanked the stationmaster for his hospitality.

It took what seemed a very long time for the other passengers to finish breakfast, and clean themselves up. Thomas was allowed to make himself comfortable in the stationmaster's favourite armchair, and to read a comic that he found on the sideboard. As he did so a parrot flew around the room several times and landed on Thomas's shoulder, nibbling his ear, much to his annoyance. The parrot then suddenly started squawking and screeching, and clearly uttered, 'You are a liar; you are a liar.' This made Thomas jump a little in the chair, which made the parrot fly off and return to its perch.

'Oh don't take any notice of the bird, it's always misbehaving itself,' said Roberta, returning from the kitchen after performing one of her duties.

'Don't be afraid, my little friend,' interrupted David, mistaking Thomas's guilty look for one of fright.

Thomas wondered if the parrot was intelligent enough to know that he was making up stories to explain his presence in the abandoned train. Furthermore, what did David mean when he said "my little friend"? It was an expression his father and younger sister used a lot at home, but surely it was just a coincidence that David used it as well? Just then, Richard the stationmaster spoke.

'Since you people are still stranded (both the railway and the roads are still blocked), there is no alternative but for you to stay here with us until the relief train arrives, probably sometime this afternoon. We will make sure you eat a decent meal. My wife will be only too pleased to cook you all dinner, and may I suggest we go into the lounge where there is a nice warm fire? We could just sit and talk or else play some games, such as dominoes and cards, but that is up to you. I think it a bit of an imposition to expect us to help you to free the engine and carriages from the track; they are frozen solid to the track. There are icicles about two feet long hanging from parts of the train. The rest of the staff is busy trying to thaw out the points.'

Bernard asked if he could light his pipe, to which the others agreed, except for Thomas as he hated anyone who smoked, although he managed to keep his thought to himself. Bernard and David offered to assist Roberta to clear up the dirty dishes and then play games afterwards if time permitted. Ivor would remain behind to rest his injured foot. At times Thomas could hear his name mentioned and he got the impression that a debate was taking place concerning what was to be done with him. He wished he could find out more but the fact that Ivor was still there prevented him from doing this.

The chores having been duly completed, the group returned to the lounge to play games, while Richard and Roberta stayed in the kitchen and started to prepare dinner. It was decided that dominoes would be the first game that was to be played, since Thomas would know the rules. Before the games started, however, David whispered in Thomas's ear so that the others could not hear, 'I hope you don't become silly and start throwing the dominoes around if you don't win. This is someone else's house, remember.' Thomas was quite taken aback by this, as he knew himself to be a poor loser, and how did David know that he would be likely to throw the dominoes around if he lost the game? Thomas decided that he had better behave himself and not lose his patience.

*

The games went well, and Thomas won a few games after all. He also learnt a lot of card games that he never knew before, which made the time pass quite quickly. Lunch time came and went, and some of those present again offered to clear up afterwards and wash the dirty dishes. Richard informed them that the train would arrive at about 4 o'clock, although it would be dark again by then, since it was a winter's day.

When the relief train eventually arrived, two other passengers showed up, completely unaware that the railway officially closed the day before. The group finally bade farewell to the stationmaster and his wife and then made their way to the platform once more. It was obvious that the railway staff had made a stupendous effort in clearing the snow away from the platform and the immediate area to make the ground safer to walk on. At the opposite platform stood the relief train with a black pannier tank similar to the one that was still frozen to the rails. The passengers were instructed to cross the line very carefully across a boarded path made up of wooden sleepers, freshly brushed and cleaned. Thomas noticed that there was another signal box on this side of the line, which was larger than the one they had all slept in, and wondered why this was not used for their needs. The engine gave a toot to hurry the passengers along, and a different guard saw them safely aboard one of the maroon-coloured carriages, before waving a green flag to signal the driver. With a final loud whistle and cheers all around, the train gradually moved forward with a jerk, and it was off.

The group was strangely quiet as the train travelled along a wooded valley still white with snow. Thomas could see that the line crossed a few lofty viaducts and cuttings before passing a short platform in the woods. After such an adventure, there was a sense of anti-climax and of sadness, because this was the last passenger train of all to traverse the pleasant branch line, which had served the local population for eight decades. The train stopped for a little while in another station, and behind one of the platforms were sidings in which stood wagons.

The train then moved off again, and went under a bridge before cautiously joining the main line into Linemouth. At last Thomas recognised where he was.

There was a river alongside the track and a creek to the other side, which he didn't think existed. He thought that there was now a road in its place. David suggested to him that it might be a good idea that the two of them go outside of the compartment to the corridor of the train for a better view of the river. David then said to Thomas something that he thought was remarkable.

'I know you were lying when you said you were locked in a crate. You will be in a lot of trouble when you get back to Linemouth because the police will be waiting. They will want to interview you and arrange transport to take you back to Travelstild, and you don't want that as I know you don't live there. I know you are from the future, and I will help you to get back to where you belong if you listen to what I have to say.'

Thomas was really surprised at this statement from David, although he did let slip several times that he had suspicions about his reasons for being present on numerous occasions. Together, the two hatched up a plan on how to escape from the others when the train arrived at Linemouth station.

'You will pretend you have some belongings to collect from the left luggage lockers. When you find the lockers, go behind them, and you will find a brown wooden door in the corner by a telephone kiosk. Go in that door and close it behind you. Do not be afraid and just trust me. Now here is the key for the door. Leave it in the lock when you go in, and I will pick it up later.'

Thomas thought that he had better do as David said; after all, he had nothing to lose, and everything to gain, although he was somewhat apprehensive.

David had been very good to him throughout this adventure, so why shouldn't he trust him? The two returned to the compartment for the remainder of the journey, which was not very long, for after a few minutes the train drew into Linemouth station. David and Thomas managed to put some distance between them and the others, and after being admitted through the ticket barriers, he spotted the left luggage lockers. 'Quickly,' whispered David, as some newspaper reporters moved towards them.

Thomas ducked and swerved around the advancing crowd of people. Being rather small, he could escape their clutches. Behind the lockers he spotted the bright red telephone kiosk and then that all-important brown door. With a final lunge he unlocked the door and threw himself into what seemed to him to be a broom cupboard. As he shut the door a white mist enveloped him and it became thicker and thicker. *Oh no*, he thought to himself. *Am I going to be knocked out again?* He heard banging on the outside of the door and Thomas felt himself becoming dizzy as he was sucked into a vortex of swirling fog and snow. He heard the voices outside the door become more hushed and then they faded altogether as he appeared to land with a bump on a wooden floor.

CHAPTER 3

The Day That Didn't Exist

Thomas found himself sitting on an uncomfortable floor and reached out to steady himself on what seemed to him to be a low wooden table. The white mist gradually dissipated and he realised that he was in his model railway room. He had arrived back home, but what date was it? In his hand was the newspaper from 1962. Somehow he must have remembered to keep it with him as he ran into the cupboard at the station. He rubbed his eyes, and realised he was very tired. He must think clearly while he was still reasonably alert, before he fell asleep in the model railway room. From the corner of his eye he thought he could see the model engines and little people moving about of their own accord, but he dismissed this as he decided what to do next. Thomas concealed the newspaper under the staging of the railway, crept downstairs to his bedroom, and climbed into his bed. *That's strange*, he thought to himself. *I'm wearing pyjamas and not the outdoor clothes I had on before, and how did I manage to bring the newspaper back?* Before he could think of a reason for this Thomas went off to a deep sleep.

*

Thomas was woken by the sound of his mother's voice calling from downstairs.

'Hurry up; it's time to get up. We are going into town soon to look for bargains in the sales.' Her voice became louder, and the door to his bedroom opened. 'Good grief,' his mother said as the she came into the room. 'What have you been doing?'

Thomas then realised that his sheets were in a somewhat dishevelled state and that his hands were dirty. 'Why is your face so black? Have you been down a coal mine?' He could only reply that he had been crawling about in the loft the night before looking for something after the others had gone to bed. His mother replied that Thomas ought to have a bath since he was very dirty, and then have breakfast afterwards. This would make dinner late, and so upset her plans for the rest of the day.

'Don't forget, I want to do all the washing today, because it is so unlucky to do washing on New Year's Day.' A shudder then went through his body.

That's strange, he thought. *I'm sure it was the 29th yesterday. If what Mum says is true it is the 31st of December, or New Year's Eve today. What happened to the 30th of December?*

Thomas felt refreshed after his bath, and went downstairs for his breakfast. His two sisters had already eaten, and were watching the television when he walked into the lounge. They were very surprised to see him get up so late in the morning. The day wore on as it usually did in the household, and a lot of the time Thomas wanted to go back to sleep again. Somehow life wasn't as exciting as the experience he had just gone through. He wished he could tell his parents what had happened to him, but knew that they wouldn't believe him. The whole thing seemed so incredible, and the thought of going back into the railway room concerned him. Thomas was afraid of what might happen to him, so he thought he had better keep away from the loft.

The rest of the family noticed that he was unusually quiet, and asked what was on his mind, but he didn't answer, as he didn't hear them. His thoughts were still elsewhere. His mother told him that the family would now go into the city centre in the afternoon, since by now it was nearly midday. The family might as well have dinner in. 'Your father intends watching the fireworks on the seafront later tonight, if anyone is interested,' his mother said, just as he began to drift off to sleep again. In order to stay awake, Thomas went over the events of the last few days in his mind. He realised that December 30th did not exist to him as it would normally, but only as what took place at Fackleton. He distinctly remembered December 29th at home and waking up on New Year's Eve. He felt that it would be in his own interests if he did not tell anyone else of his experiences, and to remain silent about the whole affair. Luckily, Thomas would be fully occupied tagging along with the rest of the family for the rest of the day.

The only exciting thing that happened to Thomas was the fireworks at midnight on Linemouth promenade. The afternoon was spent looking around the shops, and a lot of the day was taken up by meal times. In the evening Michael took Thomas to the town centre and promenade to see the fireworks. The rest of the family did not seem at all interested in the festivities, but at least Thomas thought he had something to look forward to in the evening to break up an otherwise boring day. When the time came to leave he could hardly wait, and it turned out that he must have been one of the youngest and the smallest individuals on the seafront that night. When the firework display was over, Thomas and his father made their way back to the car, which took a considerable time. It appeared to him that it took a lot longer going home that it did getting to the promenade in the first place. It was about one o'clock in the morning when he finally got to bed again. By then it was 1st January, and the start of a New Year. *What lies in store for me now?* Thomas asked himself as he drifted off to sleep once more.

*

The bright sunshine through his bedroom window woke Thomas up. There was the familiar blue wallpaper to ease him into a state of alertness at the start of another new day. He glanced at his calendar to make sure of the date, only to see that the previous year's was still hanging on the wall. He knew that it was unlucky to hang a new calendar up before it was due, so he still wasn't sure what the real date was. Thomas did not know what to expect after his adventure, and needed to confirm the correct date later in the day to make sure that he did not lose another day in his life. He also realised that sooner or later he must pay another visit to the model railway, otherwise his father would become suspicious of why he wasn't showing any interest in it. Somehow he must summon up enough courage to enter the railway room once again. He decided that after breakfast and watching his favourite television channel, this is what he would do. The family would not be doing very much, at least in the morning, and as usual he was one of the first to get out of bed. He got his own breakfast and watched television for a time, keeping the volume very low, so as not to wake the rest of the family, as he was still the only person awake. However, Thomas soon became bored with the programmes on the television: the cartoons that were being screened were repeats he had seen only a few days before, and he did not want to watch anything else. He therefore decided to dress and pay a visit to the model railway.

Thomas opened the door of the railway very slowly, as he was understandably somewhat apprehensive of what might happen next. At least there was no white mist, so he felt around for the light switch that was on the wall alongside the door. Everything appeared to be normal, so Thomas cautiously went inside. The various models were just as he left them before his adventure into the past, and the box containing the miniature people was still on the floor with the contents scattered all around. Some of the tiny people were on the model itself, which Thomas thought was strange. He wondered how they got there if the rest of them were on the floor, and some of them were in some odd positions, such as in the actual engines and carriages. Thomas knew that he didn't put them there. He also observed that the Great Western part of Bridcup station resembled that of Fackleton in his adventure. There were two platforms which served to accommodate a passing loop, a bridge over the railway and two signal boxes, one of which resembled the larger one at Fackleton. It was also in a different location, being situated at the opposite end of the platform.

Thomas then tried out the model by switching on the controller as he would normally, and everything appeared the same as usual. The small black tank engine that he called "Black Thomas" was always the most reliable, even if it was the oldest, and it sped along the track just at had always done in the past. However, something distracted him from his task of controlling the model as a movement in the far end of the loft attracted his attention. One of the miniature figures that had been upset on the floor was becoming larger and larger before his very eyes, and Thomas was by now staring at this phenomenon with his mouth wide open in amazement. In fact, Thomas had to pinch himself to make sure he was really awake, and gripped onto one of the model supports to stop himself from fainting. He wanted to run away, but he just froze dead still as this strange person grew, and took on a more realistic appearance. Thomas remembered that the box of small people had been scattered of its own accord, and that the person who now stood before him resembled Headeroonie Bill, the guard from the snowbound train at Fackleton.

'Do not be afraid,' said Headeroonie Bill.

Once again Thomas became petrified at the experience of a person manifesting out of nothing. After all, who wouldn't be? Headeroonie Bill sensed that the little boy was very alarmed and put one hand on his arm and the other on his shoulder, patting it very gently.

'Don't you remember me? I have travelled forward in time, just as you travelled back in time the other day. When your father built this model railway he unleashed a spiritual force that you and your family could not possibly understand. Perhaps one day you will be able to grasp what powerful forces have been set free within this little room. In the meantime, just trust me. I want to be your friend and mentor. If it helps I can disappear as quickly as I appear, I have special powers that enable me to detect when someone is approaching, so I can become very small again within no time at all. I will protect you always from anything untoward that might take place in here. This will be our little secret.'

With that last statement Headeroonie Bill gradually became smaller and smaller until he resumed his original size. Thomas picked the small figure up very gently and laid him out on the one of the platforms of the main station.

'Perhaps I should put all these small models away in the plastic container, and tidy this place up.'

This was contrary to his normal behaviour, as his father was annoyed with Thomas because he could be very untidy at times. On this occasion Thomas thought that he should clear up any evidence of what had happened to him. His mother was already somewhat suspicious of how he became so dirty whilst in bed, so it would be better to cover his tracks. With that thought he caught sight of the newspaper he had brought back with him, and started to read the front page. Sure enough, it was dated December 1962, which came as a relief since he still wondered if he had dreamt all this up, and this was positive proof that he had indeed travelled backwards in time.

I had better hide this paper away from everybody, he thought to himself, pushing it further back under the staging of the model railway.

Just as he did this Michael came into the railway room and said, 'Oh, there you are. I have been looking for all over the house trying to find you; I thought you had lost interest in the model railway, which would be a shame after all the hard work I have put in trying to build it. I thought I heard voices in here. Have you been talking to yourself?'

Thomas was quite taken aback by this question. He realised that Headeroonie Bill's voice must have carried further than he thought as he glanced down on the railway where he had placed him.

'Well, I suppose I might have been thinking out loud for a time concerning what to do next building the railway. I was thinking of doing some alterations to the track layout, and perhaps put some extra points in just past Gordon's Cutting.'

Michael did not believe Thomas and replied, 'I didn't think it was your voice that I heard, and it sounded like someone else's, unless it was distorted by all the insulation in the loft. Yes, perhaps that was it.' Thomas gave an inward sigh of relief, as it seemed he was off the hook again, but for how much longer could he get away with it?

'As it happens I was hoping to do some work on the railway over the Christmas holidays, and I was thinking about doing some alterations on the same lines, if you excuse the unintended pun. If you like, perhaps we could install some extra sidings where you suggested, and even a little station out of some scraps of wood. We could call this area Pit Hole Quarry Siding since it will have to be a dead end. We have some spare track left over, but we will to buy some more points like you said. This depends on how much I can afford after all the expense of Christmas. I have plenty of time on my hands, as I don't have to go back to work for a few days.'

The days passed by and father and son worked on the model, improving the layout into the quarry sidings, and adding scenery, using plaster left over from jobs around the house. Some water-based paints were left behind from a toy box and this was used to make the scenery more realistic, and it was certainly an improvement on the bare white plaster. The work was carried out in relatively short periods of time over several days until Christmas was nearly over. Twelfth Night came; the day that the decorations should be taken down, otherwise it would be unlucky, according to superstition.

In the meantime, Thomas had completely forgotten about the newspaper he had concealed under the staging of the railway. This was fairly typical of him, as he often forgot where he put things. This time, however, it was to prove disastrous to him.

As Michael was putting the Christmas decorations away, with the help of Thomas, he noticed the old newspaper that had been hidden away for about a week. As he took it out, he of course noticed the date, and called out to him, 'Have you seen this old newspaper before? It dates from when the former Great Western Railway branch line closed in the midst of the hard winter in the early sixties. I didn't even know I had this paper, and anyway, I usually keep all the newspapers together in the bookshelves, and not crumpled up under here. Apart from being creased, it is intact, and the strange thing is, it has not turned yellow with age. Do you know anything about it?'

Thomas at once regretted not hiding it away properly, and his face turned red with embarrassment. A long silence followed during which he still searched for an answer.

Michael was becoming aware that he was trying to conceal something about the paper, and felt sure that he knew something about it, but wasn't going tell.

'Well?' said Michael in an annoyed tone. 'Didn't you hear what I said?'

This stirred Thomas into a response at last.

'I don't know, perhaps you've had it for all this time and just forgot about it.'

'I don't think so,' replied Michael. 'I know what I've got, and certainly don't remember this. There has been something fishy going on here over the last few days. You still haven't explained why you woke up the other day all dirty, and I am going to get the bottom of this one day. In the meantime, you can help me finish putting all these decorations away.'

The pair worked steadily away, but little was said between them, and the atmosphere remained tense. Alison, Thomas's younger sister, came to help towards the end, when most of the work had been done, but it did help to relieve some of the pressure. Thomas was thinking all the time about how to explain himself, and came to the conclusion that honesty was the best policy, but who would possibly believe him? If only Michael would forget to question him any further.

Luckily for Thomas another meal followed, and other family members were talking about something entirely different, providing a diversion, if only for a short time. A quick exit from the dining room was called for, but it seemed to Thomas that his father was keeping an eye on him the whole time. His chance came when his father went out to the kitchen to make a pot of tea. Thomas grasped the opportunity to slip quietly away, and ran upstairs as quickly as he could. Instinctively, he continued up the stairs until he reached the model railway. There was still enough space under the staging for him to hide, so this he did, completely covering himself with dustsheets and blankets.

Thomas felt safe, at least for a short time, which seemed all too brief, for after a short interval the door of the railway room opened and in climbed Michael.

'Hello, I know you're hiding in there, son. It's no use hiding away; I've come to find out the truth.'

Thomas shuddered when he heard this, and this

gave him away, for the dustsheets and blankets moved sufficiently for his father to notice him.

'You can come out now,' said Michael, as he walked over to where Thomas was hiding and grasped him by his arm, pulling him out in quite a rough manner.

The pair of them started to move out of the railway area, but as they did so Thomas accidentally tugged at a wire underneath the model. A strange thing then happened, for Headeroonie Bill, the guard, became bigger and bigger before their very eyes. Thomas had seen this before, but of course Michael had not and he nearly collapsed with shock.

The room filled with the white swirling mist, which became a vortex, sucking up both father and son. The mist then assumed the shape of a ghostly face and uttered a strange phrase, 'Mana, Mana,' through its large toothless mouth. Michael and Thomas were both sucked into the large cavernous aperture, and fell down, down, down into what appeared to be oblivion.

CHAPTER 4

Thomas Meets the Preservationists

Thomas and Michael found themselves sitting in a bus shelter in a large car park, which was almost empty. Michael was huddled in a corner with his head bowed, and was asleep. On the ground was a picnic hamper that was always used for family outings and Thomas thought how strange it was that it got there in the first place. In the distance a black diesel engine was attached to a single red and cream carriage and a guard's van and stood at a short platform.

Thomas was wondering why it was such a warm sunny day, and not the dark, wet, dreary one that he left behind. Michael gave out a snore and woke up. He rubbed his eyes and shuffled about a little in the seat.

'Oh yes, this is why we came here. We are going to travel on the train over there after we have eaten our dinner. It only travels for a short distance and comes back again, and doesn't run to a strict timetable.'

Thomas thought that this was strange, as the last thing he remembered, Michael was about to question him over an old newspaper and now it seemed that he had forgotten all about it. Furthermore, they were in a totally different time and place. It also seemed odd that the rest of the family were not around; his mother and two older sisters did not appear to be anywhere.

The two of them finished eating their dinner, packed their belongings away, made their way out of the car park, and crossed the road to the station. Up the ramp, they walked into the main station building.

'We have to buy our tickets now,' said Michael, breaking the silence. 'I suggest we look at the displays, because there is still some time to wait until the next train. Stay here while I go over to the counter.'

Thomas did as he was bid, noticing that there were a lot of posters, with photographs and a few small maps. He was able to see that this was a preserved railway trying to re-open a section of the railway line that once went between Linemouth and Broken Castle. Then Thomas suddenly realised that this was the same railway line both in his model at home in the loft, and also the one he went back in time to in the blizzard of 1962!

He looked at more of the items for sale and noticed that the man at the till had a nameplate on the counter. The name appeared to be very strange, being Malter Witty, and just as his father approached the shopkeeper said, 'I can see you are interested in my name. This is the one I was christened with, strange that it may appear. I have been told I have ideas above my standing in life and having tried many occupations I have to settle for being a helper for the railway. I tried to write a book once but it ran out of steam and had to be shunted into a siding. On a good day I could write four or five chapters but now I cannot write a single word. I gave up twelve years ago and now in all this time my son has finished both his school and university career and is on a gap year in a foreign country. Now how may I help you?'

The pair looked at each other in disbelief at the man divulging so much information without being prompted. Was there a hidden meaning in all this?

Eventually, after some thought, Michael enquired about buying tickets and uttered, 'I observe that you have a large bag of model railway ballast which we require, but why is it called transportation gravel?'

'Oh, it's the last one we have and it is reduced in price due to the misspelling.'

'Who is Miss Pelling?' asked Thomas.

'Why, don't be impertinent boy,' replied the shop keeper. 'Are you taking the Michael because of my name?'

'How come you know my Christian name?' said Thomas's father.

'Enough of this,' bellowed Malter. 'Let's start again, shall we? I suppose you still want to buy return tickets and the bag of transportation gravel.'

'Yes please,' replied Thomas and Michael

simultaneously. 'We are sorry about all the fuss,' they added.

Malter appeared to be placated by this and the transaction was completed without any further ado. 'Please make your way to the platform. The next train will be here very shortly and the new terminus is at Cheesemore. You can remain on the train if you wish, or have a look around. Should you miss the last train it is only two miles to walk back on the shared cycle track. Your driver today will be Serendipity Moonplast and the fireman Augustus Flagitt. Have a pleasant and memorable day.'

Strange names all these people have, thought Thomas, *and why mention their names at all?*

Father and son made their way outside of the shop and towards the awaiting train. Standing by the engine were two men dressed in blue boiler suits, and to Thomas they looked exactly like each other and also the shopkeeper. When Thomas conveyed this observation to Michael, he replied, 'Don't be so silly. You have been acting very silly for some time now. They are so very different in appearance. It is how you perceive things.'

Thomas felt very aggrieved by this but chose not to say anything. It was obvious to him that these people concerned with the railway, and indeed all the passers-by, seemed so unreal. The clothes were normal but the people themselves appeared strange, more like the tiny figures in the model railway. This was also evident inside the shop, but the moment they got outside things seemed to change even more, and the whole scene was changing in front of his very eyes. How this was not clear to Michael was beyond

Thomas's comprehension, and the latter was becoming more apprehensive with each passing moment. At last his nerve gave way, and tugging at his father's sleeve, he uttered, 'Dad I want to go home because I am very scared of this place.'

Michael replied, 'Don't be so silly, son. I really don't know why are you are making such a fuss. I have come here for a reason since the railway is open one day a week. It relies on a volunteer workforce you know, and furthermore I do not have much time to come as I am at work all day.'

The pair made their way along the platform towards the engine, where the driver and fireman were standing looking just as strange as everyone else, at least to Thomas if not his father. Just then, a loud voice bellowed behind them, 'Hello there. I am Headeroonie Bill, your guard for this trip. I especially like waving red flags to tell the train to stop if required, and green ones for it to depart. This is when all the passengers are in the train and the doors are shut, according to our operating regulations.'

This person also appeared weird to Thomas, and looked very similar to the character in the model railway he had met very recently. All of them on this potty railway looked as though they were made of plastic, with all their features smudged.

All of a sudden these three people burst into a strange song. It went:

Barnpotting across the Luniverse in a barnmobile and with Thomas Pigglewick.

Barnpotting across the Luniverse, always going backwards never in reverse.

48

The "always going backwards" was sung in a low tone of voice, and the "never in reverse" was sung in a high-pitched screech.

With this, Thomas went into a state of alarm, protesting at his father the strange behaviour of these even stranger people, though to his consternation Michael had not seen or heard anything at all!

'Ah,' said Michael. 'It appears that it is time to board the train. The guard is holding the door open on the last carriage, which is a brake third composite with the guard's portion to the rear. It is the coach painted red and cream and not the normal maroon livery. It is good to see a Great Western Prairie tank at the front of the train, don't you think? It's just like the good old days. Why are you looking so pale, son? Everything appears to be normal. Come on, let's find a seat, the guard is getting impatient and wants the train to leave.'

With that, the pair got in and the door was closed behind them. This was followed by a whistle from the train, and the release of steam, after which the train started to move slowly forward with the grinding of wheels against the somewhat rusty rails.

'Well young man,' exclaimed Headeroonie Bill without any warning and making Thomas nearly jump out of his seat, which he had only occupied a few moments before. 'Perhaps you would like to come with me and I will show you how the guard's van operates, if your father approves.'

'Of course,' replied Michael. 'Perhaps this will keep you occupied for a while and maybe a little distraction will divert you from this present spell of silliness.'

Thomas thought that this was an obscure thing to say and was not sure what this meant, only it seemed apparent that his father wanted his son out of the way for a time. He arose from his seat and followed the guard to the rear door of the carriage, which was normally out of bounds to members of the general public. Headeroonie Bill unlocked the door with one of his many keys secured to a loop on his belt with a long chain. The poor unfortunate child was gently pushed into the dark surroundings of the guard's private quarters, which was swiftly illuminated by the pressing of a light switch.

'Good. We are alone now. I would like to explain a few things to you. It seems to me that you possess magical powers, otherwise you would not have brought back a newspaper from 1962 into the present time. Now don't interrupt, I know that you did this due to my friends from your model railway. You probably know me as Headeroonie Bill from your loft, and there are other people from that structure here as well. Now I want your help to get us back where we belong using that packet of transportation granules you have. If you use it properly you can come back with us too. Don't worry about your father. We will erase his memory, and you won't lose any time in your life.'

As he talked, Headeroonie Bill prepared a drink for Michael, using ingredients from various wild flowers from railway embankments and allotments adjoining different stations. This concoction was prepared a long time before, in case of emergencies, and was guaranteed to give the victim a long and peaceful sleep.

'Now take this back to your seat and give it to your father. In case he gets suspicious, here is one for you without the secret ingredients that looks very similar but is totally harmless. Make sure he drinks it all and then soon he will fall asleep, then we can enjoy ourselves without him knowing a single thing. Don't worry, you are perfectly safe and will not come to any harm. All of us need to go back to your model railway because there is a chasm in time which means that somehow we ended up here and we do not really belong.'

Thomas seemed to be utterly confused by all this but agreed to help, realising that something was drastically wrong with these strange people. He thought he could be in great danger if he did as he was told, but he could be in even greater danger if he disobeyed. As Thomas was pondering over his options he realised that every move he made was being watched by Headeroonie Bill as he made his way back to his seat. He gave the drink to his father, making sure it was the one that was drugged.

In no time at all Michael gave a loud snort and slumped back fast asleep, Thomas observing that the short train passed the sidings, followed a bridge, and finally through a deep cutting. Everything appeared to be two dimensional and very unreal. Headeroonie Bill had by now sat next to Thomas and said, 'When we reach our destination at Wooded Valley we will make our way back to your model. What you have to do is give the bag of transportation granules a tight squeeze at the same time as myself, and in a short time we will be somewhere else. There will be a special reception for you when we arrive.'

In no time at all the train reached the terminus and all the passengers disembarked except for Michael, who was still fast asleep. To Thomas's great surprise, grouped around the outside of the train on the very short platform were not only Headeroonie Bill but also Augustus Flagitt, Serendipity Moonplast, and Malter Witty.

'Don't worry about your father,' said Headeroonie Bill. 'He will be perfectly alright and will awake when we depart. The real people will drive the train back but we must leave ourselves with your help, Thomas.'

The group then formed a circle holding hands, with Thomas in the middle, and started chanting the strange song again:

Barnpotting across the Luniverse, in a barnmobile and with Thomas Pigglewick.

Barnpotting across the Luniverse, always going backwards, never in reverse.

They sang this silly chant several times over until Headeroonie said to Thomas, 'Now squeeze the bag of transportation granules and hold on to it very tightly.'

With that, a white swirling mist descended around them, and sucked the group upwards at a fast speed, at which point Thomas passed out.

CHAPTER 5

Back to the Model Railway and an
Introduction to the Little People

When Thomas became conscious he was lying on his back facing upwards to what appeared to be the roof of the loft. He moved his head from side to side and observed three of the characters from the preserved railway along with other characters that he did not recognise. He thought that all of the figures were asleep until he heard a shuffling behind him which made him get to his feet. There was Headeroonie Bill in the process of waking. On looking around, he made out the cardboard buildings of the railway platform made by his father. This made him realise that he was back in the model railway but this time he was very much smaller, because he was the same size as all the other figures!

Suddenly there was a voice amongst the array of fallen toy figures which belonged to Headeroonie Bill.

'Hello Thomas, you are known as Tonkas here. Don't worry about your normal life, it is frozen to where you left it and your dad will forget everything. We need your help with something that I will explain later.'

As this conversation was going on the other members of the preservationists appeared, which gave Thomas a start. *I had better remember my new name*, he thought.

'Let's tell Tonkas about how we all came to exist,' said Augustus Flagitt.

'Yes, what a good idea,' replied Serendipity Moonplast, 'though it's a long story.'

'Well it seems I will be here for a long time,' answered Tonkas.

The group then decided to adjourn to the waiting room of the Great Western platform where it would be warmer and more comfortable.

Headeroonie Bill opened the proceedings by acting as the self-appointed chairman, though he always seemed to take on the leading role anyway.

'I would like to tell Tonkas about our group if that's alright with the rest of you,' and the others nodded in consent.

'Very well then,' he continued. 'Many of us descended from the union of Brutus Maximus, a large dog, and Mandy, a large cat, and we are known as the five kittendogs, even though in no way do we resemble either cats or dogs. This must be due to some freak of nature. You have met all four of us, the others are called The Alisose, Mareekoid, Sylvate, and Mickel.

'Tonkas was the only missing one of our band until today, so this is why we wanted you, as Thomas, to come back with us. Now that we are complete we will continue in our quest of finding Mandy and Brutus, who both are missing. The saying around here is that both disappeared during a battle with our enemies, some huge creatures that look something like woodlice. Brutus remains as a ghostly figure who sometimes says, "Mana, Mana." We must find The Alisose, Mareekoid, and Mickel. We left them behind before our visit to the preserved railway.'

Tonkas thought to himself, *I am losing my senses here, first a change of name and now all this nonsense.*

At this point Serendipity spoke. 'We ought to try and look for them at our parents' mansion; they could be doing some repairs after the battle with the giant killer woodlice.'

Tonkas again considered, *How on earth would there be room for a mansion house, even a model one, inside our loft? All we had room for was the main station with a few cardboard buildings, some plastic houses and just one short stretch of road.*

With that thought, Headeroonie Bill again took the leading role and headed the group out of the waiting room, and the Great Western station. They then followed the approach road over the bridge with its view of the tracks, and into open countryside. The longer the party walked, the more realistic the surroundings appeared to Tonkas. This was exactly the opposite to what had happened before at the preserved railway. The scenery seemed to be more normal as in real life; there were even birds singing and a slight breeze was present. There was no room for all of this in the model railway at home, and this was rapidly changing into a real world!

The group of characters then approached a dilapidated barn at the end of a rough track.

'Ah, there it is!' exclaimed Headeroonie Bill as he opened the large wooden door of the barn. Within this ramshackle construction was an even more peculiar mode of transport. 'Here is our mobile which will get us to our destination for the night. We call it our barnmobile because it is always kept in a barn, either here or the other barn at the mansion.'

Malter was the first to open the driver's door and to start the engine.

'That's a relief,' he said as the engine made a loud clanking noise when it was eased out of the building. The vehicle had been designed and built by The Alisose and it was adaptable for railway tracks as well as the road. The vehicle also had retractable wings so it could actually fly as well! The front of this strange machine looked exactly the same as the rear, having both headlights and taillights, and with engines at both ends.

Malter chose the wings as the means of propulsion as he pulled on a lever under the dashboard. 'Quick, get in folks, before this contraption takes off and leaves you behind. It will get dark before long and it will become more difficult to find our way to our destination. Flying is the fastest way of transport, you know.'

With that command the others all got in and sat in the three rows of seats, just as the vehicle lifted itself off the ground in a vertical ascent. Enough height was gained to clear the surrounding trees. This gave a very good view of the countryside below, with its rough grass and brown bracken mixed with granite boulders and tors. Intertwined were peat bogs and though not evident from the air, the green vegetation and brown reeds gave an indication of the boggy ground.

Malter then exclaimed, 'Look, there is our mansion on the horizon next to the clump of trees, and I can see the barnmobile garage.'

'Good,' replied Headeroonie Bill. 'I was feeling a little sick; I prefer to have both my feet on the ground. Hurry up Malter, I cannot wait to get home.'

Malter released his pressure on the accelerator pedal to slow the vehicle, resulting in a violent lurch. Most of the group shot backward in their seats, but fortunately the head restraints prevented them from possible injury. There was some benefit in the sudden increase in speed, however, as the mansion was soon reached without any mishap, and the vehicle landed on the gravel drive at the front of the building. Before the group could get out they were greeted by The Alisose, Mareekoid, Sylvate, and Mickel.

The Alisose said, 'I hope you have looked after my latest invention, I have spent a long time building it.'

The passengers quickly disembarked, some of them polishing areas of the bodywork with any items of clothing close to hand, as if they were making fun of the last comment. Headeroonie Bill then drove the empty barnmobile to the rear of the mansion where there were garages and stables.

'I am putting the car thingy away for the night and will enter through the tradesman's entrance. I will see you all later in reception room 2b, where we will continue our meeting.'

Quite a long period of time elapsed before the group finally congregated after they had washed and freshened themselves. Headeroonie Bill took his usual place at the head of the table and acted as the self-appointed chairman once more. 'I suggest we tell Tonkas about our history, especially concerning the battle with the giant killer woodlice and the subsequent disappearance of your beloved parents, Mandy and Brutus.'

The others signalled their agreement.

'Very well then,' said Headeroonie Bill. 'It's only fair that Tonkas knows something of our history. He knows about the situation regarding Mandy and Brutus, but I will explain about the battle with the giant killer woodlice in greater detail later on. I doubt if Tonkas knows about kittendogs and how we all became inventors at the local Training Academy. The big boss is something of a despot and she is commonly known as She Who Must Be Obeyed or sometimes as the Big Fat Dragoness. I think she sent the giant killer woodlice after us, when one of our experiments went wrong in the laboratories in the top floor of the college.'

'Yes,' butted in Mickel. 'I assume she is jealous of our achievements and wanted us out of the way.'

'Perhaps this is true,' replied Headeroonie Bill. 'Please don't interrupt for the moment, otherwise l will lose concentration and forget what I was about to say.'

'I am very sorry,' replied Mickel. 'Please continue.'

'Thank you,' continued Headeroonie Bill. 'I was about to explain about our own inventiveness. As I said before, Tonkas knows nothing about this and must feel confused to say the least. What do you say, Tonkas?'

'Well, yes,' added Tonkas. 'I cannot understand what is going on and I feel very tired. It has been a long day, but please tell me some background detail. This will help me feel happier and will enable me to sleep better tonight. Please tell me about the battle and omit the invention side of things for now.'

'Ok, that seems a good idea,' they all said as one voice. 'Let Headeroonie Bill carry on about the details of the battle.'

The self-appointed leader then continued with his talk.

He explained that Mareekoid was the inventor of smudge bombs, which was short for Super Magnetic Uniform Dynamic Grand Energiser, and these devices neutralised the giant woodlice. This meant that the creatures became frozen to the spot and made them more vulnerable to other weaponry. The attack, at least for now, had been thwarted, but not before some damage was caused to the mansion. Hence, a working party was left behind to effect repairs.

'So this is the situation for now,' concluded Headeroonie Bill. 'It would be better if we all go to bed, but only after we all have supper.' Getting up from his chair, Headeroonie Bill rang the appropriate bell for the butler, who duly arrived. 'Decide what we all want for supper and we will reassemble in the kitchen in twenty minutes,' he added.

∗

The entire group assembled around the large table in the cold and draughty kitchen.

'We need to get on with the repairs as soon as possible,' said Mickel. 'We will have to be on the alert, and it would be better to post sentries in all the damaged rooms where the windows have been broken, and then set to work replacing broken glass and checking over the security footage to ascertain what has happened to Mandy and Brutus.'

'Good idea,' put in Tonkas. 'Though I am very tired so I don't want to be a sentry for now. Perhaps Mickel ought to be the first to volunteer since he suggested it.'

Mickel reluctantly agreed since it was not his favourite occupation, not liking to being still for long periods of time and not doing much. Tonkas got his wish and even got a bedroom to himself, much to his surprise, since he was a new member to the group. Mickel was indeed the first sentry in the kitchen, though no other sentries were needed in the mansion as no other windows were broken, just damage to the balconies where the smudge bombs were launched during the battle.

∗

Tonkas slept very soundly that night, waking up the next morning to the sound of voices from downstairs. Being a curious person, he slipped on a dressing gown conveniently left at the foot of the bed and crept on tiptoe out to the landing, and then very cautiously downstairs. However, he was not quiet enough, as the last tread on the staircase squeaked just as the kitchen door was in sight. Even though the door was closed someone must have heard the noise, as the voices stopped and the door opened slowly. Serendipity emerged and said, 'It's alright, its only Tonkas. He must have just got out of bed judging by his dishevelled appearance. Do come in, we could do with your help in looking at the video footage of the battle. With your special powers you may spot something we have missed. However, we think you should have breakfast first.'

Tonkas enjoyed a full English breakfast of fried bread, mushrooms, tomatoes, sausage, bacon, and eggs, followed by toast with marmalade, finished by coffee. He felt very full and satisfied with this, having not eaten very much the previous day. He was so gratified by his meal that he helped the cook with the washing up, though being vaguely aware that Thomas himself would not perform this task without cajolement by others. These activities were then followed by a good wash before getting dressed in freshly laundered clothes prepared by the butler.

Headeroonie Bill, Serendipity, and Augustus greeted Tonkas as he came down the stairs for the second time. This time it was Augustus who spoke first. 'One thinks it is advisable if we all go to the security room and have a set-up each to use. That way we can get through the work faster, and you never know, we might find out what actually happened during the battle.'

'That is a very good idea,' said Headeroonie Bill. 'Tonkas can have the best equipment since with his special powers he might find the solution before the rest of us. This is the camera on the roof which would have had the best view.'

Tonkas did as he was bid and settled down to a comfortable chair in the security room while the others did the same with other video tapes from other cameras situated elsewhere in and around the mansion. Tonkas found this work very tedious and as the time went very slowly his eyes became tired during the process. Nevertheless, he remained true to his task, every so often rubbing his eyes and imbibing a little water from a drinks bottle to maintain a state of alertness. The pile of video tapes diminished in height as Tonkas used the fast forward facility to great effect, as he seemed to possess a special power that enabled him to remember every image that he saw in much greater detail than anyone else could. Despite all this he observed nothing out of the ordinary and he finally reached for the last video tape, when a strange sensation came over him, as if he was about to witness something that would provide some indication of what happened in the battle.

At the very last minute of the video footage Tonkas spotted what he thought was a defect in the actual tape, but on reflection there seemed to be an apparition. On one single frame there appeared to be a large white area in front of a giant killer woodlouse, into which Mandy and Brutus disappeared, along with the woodlouse itself. Then the tape suddenly finished and Tonkas fell off the chair with shock.

When Tonkas came round he was reclining on a

couch with Headeroonie Bill, Serendipity, and Augustus standing over him applying cold wet towels to his forehead.

'What happened, dear boy? We found you lying on the floor with a chair on top of you, and how did you finish analysing all those tapes? We only managed to look at a few, and you went through the lot of them.'

Tonkas then realised what happened and related what he saw to the others in great detail.

'I told you that you had special powers, getting through all that footage yet memorising every single frame, none of us could do that. Now rest easy while we check over your findings,' said Headeroonie Bill.

Tonkas did has he was bid, using the time effectively by having a light lunch in the kitchen and getting to know the cook at the same time. After that he explored the mansion, in order to familiarise the areas that he thought were relevant to him. He got lost several times wandering around on his own, and thought he had better find his way back.

Finally, Tonkas arrived back at the security room to be greeted by a chorus from all the others he left behind. 'Ah, there you are. Where have you been all this time?' they asked as one unified voice. 'Never mind,' they added before Tonkas had a chance to reply. 'Come inside and we will tell you what we discovered when you were away.'

Headeroonie Bill, Serendipity, and Augustus then explained in great detail that they made a marker on the video tape where the occurrence happened that Tonkas described to them earlier. This related to the time elapsed and the location of the camera. Luckily this applied to the other video cameras pointed to the same location, within a little latitude to allow for any errors. There appeared to be general agreement amongst them that the white area could be a time warp, and that the voice that was heard repeatedly saying, 'Mana,' was the same Tonkas had heard before. The voice was identified as belonging to Brutus.

'We must make a plan on how to explore this area, if we find the exact location. It is getting late now and besides, we are all tired after looking at all these pictures all day.

'I think I might know where this spot is, judging by the surrounding vegetation and a peculiar-looking boulder,' said Headeroonie Bill as an afterthought.

'That boulder looks strange,' interjected Augustus. 'One knows the exact spot, but the boulder looks different in these images. It looks larger and has some markings on it that I don't recognise. On the other hand, I could be mistaken, one needs to see the real thing, doesn't one?'

'Yes,' said Headeroonie Bill. 'Let's check up on this tomorrow.' With that comment, the topic was closed and the group decided to have supper and then retire for the night.

CHAPTER 6

All About Rocks and Woodlice

The day opened with the dawn chorus of electric cuckoos from the grape trees contained in the garden. The electric cuckoos and grape trees were inventions of Mareekoid, the chief recycler of the Mandy and Brutus kittendogs. The grape trees were not really trees, but merely looked like them. The vines had grown to such an extent that the greenhouse looked like a tropical environment. Of the kittendogs, most of them had already arisen by the time Tonkas had found his way to the kitchen. Before he could eat, the other members had discussed the plan for the day; the retrieval of the boulder and tracking down the whereabouts of the giant killer woodlice. Serendipity was not too happy about this and thought this was too ambitious. It was either one or the other, he stipulated. There was not enough time for the personnel to do both, and furthermore any rain that fell overnight could wash away tracks left behind by the woodlice. Serendipity's stance annoyed Headeroonie Bill who, as usual, wanted his own way, overruling everyone else.

After breakfast and preparations for the day's activities, the group made their way from the kitchen to the garage and stables to retrieve the barnmobile, and the two Moorland ponies. The Alisose drove the car and Mareekoid the ponies with the help of Augustus, all the others getting into the car. Progress was slow as the group made its way to the battlefield, with two ponies trotting behind the car. The ponies were chosen because they were deemed more suitable for the wet, soggy ground, whereas the wheeled vehicle could get bogged down in the mud, if the conditions were not suitable.

'Perhaps I should have built the barnmobile more like a tank with its caterpillar arrangement to help us get to our destination,' said The Alisose. 'I could consider this when it is due for its service.'

'It's a bit late to think of that,' said Headeroonie Bill. 'We will have to make do with the present hardware.'

The group finally left the mansion, passing the areas of mass destruction with pieces of broken woodlice everywhere, until a glade was reached corresponding to the video footage first spotted by Tonkas.

'Ah, we have arrived,' observed Headeroonie Bill. 'Look, there is the boulder we saw earlier.'

The Alisose then revealed that the device used in navigating the barnmobile had been lost in the rush, and she was somewhat disabled by its absence.

'I call it my sense of direction gland which fits into my head,' she wailed. 'I cannot find my way around without it.'

'We will look out for it on the way back,' said Tonkas, and at that point everyone got out of the barnmobile. Headeroonie Bill was the first to get to the boulder, closely followed by Tonkas, who quickly examined it.

'Look, this writing on this large rock must mean something. Not only that, I can find out the person who did the writing, though it is very faint; I can only just see it.'

All the others quickly gathered around the object, although no one else could make out any inscription. Again, Headeroonie Bill was the first to speak, confirming what all the others thought: there was no apparent writing on the stone.

'I can definitely make something out, perhaps it is written with a pencil. This stone should be taken back to the laboratory in the mansion house as soon as possible,' ordered Tonkas.

This was followed by a great deal of chattering, Augustus taking the lead for a change. 'One must get this object to a safe place, as Tonkas said. This can only be achieved with the barnmobile since it looks so heavy, and some of us will have to walk back as there is not enough room.'

'I think we should split up and use the ponies to track the giant killer woodlice, since some of them must have survived. They were so friendly to us once, but She Who Must Be Obeyed must have turned them against us, hence the onslaught aimed at the mansion house a few days ago,' said Headeroonie Bill.

This was agreed, and so Tonkas accompanied the boulder on the back seat of the barnmobile, together with the smaller members of the group to balance the loading on the vehicle.

Mareekoid said, 'Should we continue with the barnpotting? After all, I am in the habit of disappearing on my own in search of rubbish in the hope that it can be recycled, and don't forget it was me who first coined that particular phrase. This, in my language, means the act of collecting rubbish. I also like the solitude that goes along with this activity, and could look out for any other pieces of rock and woodlice that happen to be lying around.'

Everyone was shocked and surprised that Mareekoid could actually string more than two sentences together as she was usually so silent and morose.

'Good idea,' said Tonkas. 'We might find something that could be useful to us and we ought to collect all the rock that we can find in case it has more writing on it. We could also try and find any woodlice shell and other body parts for analysing. We might find something that gives some indication of why the woodlice have turned against us.'

Another debate then followed on who would track the trail of the woodlice and who would accompany Tonkas with the boulder and rocks back to the mansion. It was decided that The Alisose would go with Tonkas since she built the barnmobile and was more familiar with the controls than anyone else.

Headeroonie Bill was to go with Mareekoid and Augustus with the two ponies, which meant that one of them would have to walk, or that one of the ponies would have to be ridden by two people. This left Serendipity, Malter, Sylvate, and Mickel also to go back to the mansion house together. However, the collection of rocks and shell had to be safely loaded on the vehicle, the boulder being the first item, which required a lot of effort. Ropes and planks provided leverage until the centre of the barnmobile was loaded with all this paraphernalia. The two separate groups then had to decide the next course of action. Headeroonie Bill was to lead the expedition to follow the trail of the giant woodlice, with Tonkas, Mickel, and The Alisose occupying the front seats of the barnmobile. The Alisose wanted to drive, but then realised that the lost sense of direction gland was a great disadvantage. Tonkas offered to take over both the driving and navigating, which made sense because of his superior observational skill.

'If we retrace our steps we may find this missing gland, which I noticed was round, black, and shiny in appearance,' cried Tonkas as the vehicle sputtered into life. A quick glance in a backward direction indicated that the other members of the kittendogs were just disappearing out of sight around a sharp bend in the track.

'Come on,' carried on Tonkas. 'If we hurry we will be back in good time to unload our finds and have plenty of time to have our dinner. With my photographic memory I hope to spot the missing sense of direction gland on the way, but we need to make haste in case the woodlice are still around.'

'But I need to find my missing sense of direction gland first,' remonstrated The Alisose. 'How can I possibly drive the barnmobile later on without it?'

'Well you know I will be driving, for the time being,' replied Tonkas. 'If you do not let me drive you will have to just change gears and I will steer. I can remember the way we came to help you. Besides, we stand a better chance of finding your sense of direction gland in this way.'

The Alisose gave a grunt and was not best pleased with Tonkas calling the barnmobile a thing. It had already proved its use in transporting the kittendogs from the railway station to the mansion house, and then the subsequent pursuit of the woodlice. Nevertheless, The Alisose reluctantly agreed with the latest demand from Tonkas in order to keep the peace, and soon they were on their way. Familiar landmarks flashed by as they sped along the track and rough ground. Tonkas had the feeling they were being watched all the time, but wasn't quite sure who or what it was. He surmised it could be the woodlice. Suddenly, he told The Alisose to stop the barnmobile. 'There it is!' Tonkas exclaimed. 'I have just spotted your lost sense of direction gland. Wait here while I go back to retrieve it.'

The barnmobile slithered to a halt, leaving deep channels in the mud as the vehicle slewed sideways. Even before it stopped Tonkas leapt out of his seat and dashed back to the sense of direction gland lying in the verge. He quickly retrieved the device and thrust it into The Alisose's lap before telling her to drive off again.

'Press the wing release button and prepare for a take-off. I think I just saw some of those woodlice,' said Tonkas.

The Alisose did as she was bid, the barnmobile rapidly gaining height, leaving the ground far below. Some creatures were spotted moving about, but were too far away to identify properly. The Alisose pressed another button on the dashboard of the car which meant that the autopilot was engaged, wrestling the control of the car away from Tonkas. This was to give her time to re-insert the sense of direction gland into the appropriate socket in the middle of her head above the eyebrows.

'That's better. I feel so much better for that. Now I know where I am going.'

'That's all very well, but we need to get back quickly. Hurry up before the woodlice see us. It's just as well they can't fly,' replied Tonkas.

'Ok,' answered The Alisose. 'I am doing the best I can, it won't be long now, and everything is under control. What about the others? If you say the woodlice are around they could be in great danger.'

'Yes, I had thought of that,' said Tonkas. 'That's why I want us to hurry up. We could unload all the stuff back home and then go back for them.'

While all this was going on Sylvate was fast asleep and snoring loudly, much to the annoyance of the passengers in the back seats, and especially Mickel. In fact, he was so displeased that he kept on nudging her foot. Sitting on the other side of her was Malter, who repeatedly nudged Sylvate with his elbow. Both these actions were having no effect, in that she still had an empty mug in her hand. *Good job there isn't any liquid in there*, thought Tonkas.

Just then, Sylvate snorted and finally dropped the mug on the floor of the car, and the noise finally woke her up where everything else had failed.

'What a relief,' exclaimed Mickel. 'I thought she would never wake up.'

'I heard that,' mumbled Sylvate as she started to cough repeatedly. 'Oh dear, I think I must have caught a cold.'

'I wish you wouldn't cough all over us,' said Mickel. 'Why don't you turn around and do all that out of the back window?'

'Alright, I will,' replied Sylvate. With that comment, she leaned out of the open rear passenger seat, forced herself over Mickel, and coughed and coughed with all her might.

There was so much force involved in this operation that the vehicle gave a sudden jerk to the left.

'If only we could capture all this surplus energy,' said Malter. 'I would like to recycle this product and use it to jet propel the barnmobile.'

'That's a good idea,' said Mickel. 'Tell Sylvate to continue coughing and sneezing and see what that does.'

This plan was put into good effect as the speed of the barnmobile increased even though it was rather jerky in places. The roof of the mansion house at last appeared, much to everyone's pleasure and excitement.

'Oh goody,' spoke Tonkas. 'We are nearly there. As soon as we get back we must unload our findings and get back to join the others.'

'Should we have a rest first?' said Sylvate. 'I am very tired with all this coughing and sneezing and feel worn out by all this activity. I ought to stay behind and look after the rocks.'

'I think this is a very good idea,' said Mickel. 'There should be at least one of us to remain, since we should keep a close eye on everything. There could be a spy in the mansion house or perhaps dark evil forces at work. For example, I don't trust the second in command of the Training Academy who looks after all the personnel. I think his name is The King, who forces people to do things they don't want to do. He is supposed to consult with staff before any decisions are made at a higher level but instead he expects them to fall into line with his own ideas. The man was an inventor himself when he was younger but transferred to management some time ago.'

'The king person sounds like a turncoat and bully to me,' interjected Sylvate.

'Yes, he represents all that is evil with the Training Academy. I am sure he has something to do with the disappearance of Mandy and Brutus and every other unfortunate event that has happened since he arrived on the scene.'

While this conversation was going on, the mansion house was now firmly in sight. The Alisose guided the barnmobile to the rear of the building using a vertical descent technique to reduce height until a firm footing was achieved. As soon as the vehicle reached solid ground everyone quickly jumped out, with Tonkas remaining behind to safeguard the valuables. He called back for Malter and Mickel who he regarded as his best friends, as well as his siblings, to provide assistance with the unloading of the important possessions. The Alisose quickly jumped out of the driver's seat and beckoned to Serendipity to do the same.

'We ought to stand guard over the barnmobile in case anything should happen to it,' said The Alisose. 'I don't want anything to happen to my beautiful car.'

'Good idea, though I think Serendipity should go inside to make sure the coast is clear and to make sure we have somewhere safe to store our findings,' stated Tonkas.

Without any delay Serendipity grabbed some broken woodlice shell and made a dash for one of the garages. 'I will hide these few items and return for more as quickly as I possibly can,' he said as he disappeared from sight. The others stood transfixed, staring at each other in complete bewilderment at the speed of this occurrence. Before anything more happened, Serendipity returned with empty cardboard boxes.

'Fill these boxes with the rocks and shells and I will take them back to a hiding place I know, and if there are not enough boxes I will get more,' said Serendipity.

The others followed these demands and fortunately all the pieces of rock and woodlice shells found their way into the boxes, except for the large boulder.

'What can we do with this large rock?' asked Tonkas, who was quite concerned about the situation.

'We have gone to a lot of trouble getting this artefact back here, and I feel this will provide answers in the quest to find Mandy and Brutus. This rock could be of great importance, more so than the pieces of woodlice shell. If you look carefully at these pieces you can see writing on the inside.'

'I saw that when I was putting the shells away,' said Serendipity. 'Some of the writing was incomplete but using different pieces of shell I could make out the whole description. This seems to be repeated on every piece of complete shell, and the entire phrase would be "Property of The Department of Dirty Tricks of the Training Academy."'

'Oh no,' replied Mickel. 'I think I know what that means. We must have been bombarded by fragments of strategic review, in the great battle of the mansion house and the giant killer woodlice. This must have been some sort of mechanism by which the king was trying to gain control over us.'

'This is sheer conjecture,' mumbled Malter, who finally had something to say. 'We should really make some progress with getting the boulder out of the car, and finding a safe place to store it. All this talking achieves very little.' With that, he stormed off to the same garage that Serendipity had found the cardboard boxes in.

After a short delay Serendipity returned with a trolley made from pram wheels, wood, and string.

'Where did you find that?' enquired Tonkas. 'I used that trolley when I was younger, playing races with a friend down a hill leading to a quarry. I haven't seen it for ages.'

'It was at the back of the garage under a tarpaulin. I found it some time ago looking for something else. I know it is strongly built because I tested it the other day and should take the weight of the boulder,' stated Malter.

'Let's get on with it then,' continued Tonkas as he grabbed the rope out of Malter's hands and steered the trolley towards the barnmobile. 'Come on you lot. Give me some help to get this large rock out of the car and on to the trolley.'

The rest of the kittendogs complied without any delay, realising the growing urgency of the situation in getting the boulder transported. 'Be careful not to rub off any of the markings from the surface, these words might explain a lot,' said Tonkas.

The trolley and boulder was whisked away and returned from whence it came back in the garage, together with the tarpaulin covering, so that no one would know anything different.

'I need a volunteer or two to stay behind to keep an eye on things while we go back for the others. I think I should go back and so should The Alisose now that her sense of direction gland is working properly. Sylvate should stay at the house because of her snoring. We want complete silence if and when we approach any giant killer woodlice. That just leaves Malter and Mickel to decide whether they go back with us or stay behind,' said Tonkas.

'I would like to stay behind with Sylvate if that's alright,' said Mickel without any delay, and Malter nodded in agreement.

'Good, that's sorted out,' replied Tonkas. 'Let's get

back to the battle site as fast as we can and pick up where we left off. The rest of you return to the mansion house before we left on our pursuit, and pretend nothing has happened. If anyone asks, you don't know where we are. Come on the rest of you. We must try to find the others while it is still daylight. Just in case we are out all night there are enough provisions to last a couple of nights in the barnmobile. I saw to that myself while no one was about, and to surprise you. I learnt to always be prepared for every eventuality as part of my school training.'

This left Tonkas himself with The Alisose as the driver, with Serendipity and Malter remaining of the kittendogs. The next challenge was the pursuit of the giant killer woodlice and the rescue of Headeroonie Bill, Mareekoid, and Augustus.

'Hurry up, The Alisose,' ordered Tonkas in a commanding way. 'We need to get back to the battle site as soon as we can, find more useful items if there are any, and then track the giant killer woodlice.'

The Alisose obeyed and soon found herself in the driving seat once more with the others in hot pursuit, Tonkas grabbing the front passenger seat. Serendipity caught up, sitting next to Malter in the back. The Alisose manoeuvred the vehicle into a clear area of the back yard where the vertical take-off engines were utilised once more. The ascent was very rapid, the passengers having little time to wave to their siblings before enough height was gained to clear the surrounding trees. Tonkas helped The Alisose find her way, even though her sense of direction gland was functioning perfectly well. They passed the place where the sense of direction gland was lost and then found again, without the distractions of Sylvate snoring and sneezing at very short intervals. The route was now becoming very familiar to the driver and navigator, and soon the barnmobile was carefully landed on a flat patch of level ground in exactly the same place as before. All the occupants got out of the vehicle, and Tonkas then brought his special powers into good use by using a different wavelength of light from his eyes, to spot a slime trail left by the woodlice.

'Look, I have found some clues to what has happened to the woodlice. They must have been injured by the smudge bombs and they have bled out this fluid, which must be the equivalent of our blood.'

'I can't see anything,' said Malter and Serendipity in unison.

'That's because you don't possess my special powers of vision,' replied Tonkas, as he retrieved three pairs of extra-vision goggles from a storage compartment of the barnmobile and handed them out to the other kittendogs. 'This should help make up for your disadvantage of you not having my superior sight,' said Tonkas in a somewhat condescending tone of voice. He continued by stating that they should have a quick look around the immediate surroundings, but not lose sight of the barnmobile.

They all agreed, although The Alisose was understandably hesitant in leaving the barnmobile unattended, so she elected to stay very close to her creation, removing the keys from the ignition as a precaution. Malter was the first to utter something when he came across another piece of woodlice shell, this time with the complete inscription, "Property of the Department of Dirty Tricks". This latest finding was carefully placed in the storage container of the barnmobile. However, nothing of any interest was found in the next few minutes so it was decided to abandon the search.

Tonkas was again the first kittendog to come up with any sort of sensible plan. 'I think it is a good idea to hide the barnmobile and proceed on foot, this way it would be a lot quieter. I have another device which will help facilitate the concealment of the machine,' as he marched over to the barnmobile and opened a flap to yet another hidden compartment. He extracted several aerosols and a large plastic sheet which he pulled over the car with the help of the others. He continued, 'These are magic cans of paint which will camouflage the car completely and no one would possibly know that it is here. Besides, this place is remote and not many people would come this way. However, before we start we had better remove the rucksacks I have stowed away. All of these contain an independent survival kit which should give us a couple days' supply. They contain tents, sleeping bags, food, in fact everything you could think of.'

Tonkas concluded his plan with a demonstration of how the spray cans worked. Indeed, they were so good that when the paint was applied it merged with the surroundings completely.

'This was an invention I made years ago,' added Tonkas. 'It makes camouflage redundant.'

'I bet any army person would not like you to say this,' said Malter.

'Well it fits the purpose on this occasion,' muttered Tonkas. 'When we are ready we can depart, and look out for hoof prints from our ponies. We can assume that Headeroonie Bill and the rest followed the woodlice, and now I have just spotted horseshoe impressions as well as the slime trail, so we must be on the right track,' added Tonkas.

Donning the extra vision goggles, the small group followed the tracks along a muddy path lined with small trees and shrubs on either side.

'We had better keep the sound of our voices down to a minimum in case we get close to the dreaded woodlice. The noise of the mud under our feet is enough to contend with,' added Tonkas.

Slowly, the kittendogs made their way along the path as the light was beginning to fade.

'I wish we had Mareekoid's electric cuckoos right now,' observed Malter. 'They are really useful in helping us kittendogs find our way around in these conditions.'

'Why didn't you say that before?' replied Tonkas. 'I will summon them right away if you like. I have my whistle in my pocket to call them. In addition, the extra vision goggles should be very useful in finding our way around.'

'Yes, I dare say,' added Malter. 'I would like to say that these cuckoos are very silent and could fly ahead of us and let us know if the woodlice are near.'

'That is a very good idea,' agreed Serendipity. 'Tonkas, would you please summon the electric cuckoos? We could do with all the help we can get.'

Tonkas, not liking to be ordered around, nevertheless took out his whistle and gave a long blast, knowing that the sound was inaudible to everyone except the cuckoos, who had a special receiver implanted in their heads by Mareekoid, the creator of these strange birdlike contraptions.

'Wait here and we will conceal ourselves in the bushes while we await the arrival of our friends,' said Tonkas.

It seemed a very long time before the mechanical birds made an appearance, by which time it was totally dark. Some of the kittendogs were beginning to shiver with the drop in temperature. Just as they started to give up hope, the electric cuckoos hovered above them, and landed on any piece of available tree branch they could find.

'Thank goodness for that,' said Serendipity. 'Now we have reinforcements. I think we should settle down here and get into our sleeping bags. The cuckoos can stand guard overnight.'

The other kittendogs agreed with this, consuming a little chocolate to provide some nourishment, and soon drifted off to sleep.

*

Malter was the first to awake, feeling a draught around his head, and realised that it was one of the cuckoos flapping its wings above his head. Malter sat up and instinctively nudged the person next to him who was The Alisose. 'Quickly, get up and rouse the others, I have a feeling that something is about to happen.'

Tonkas and Serendipity must have been disturbed because they got up at the same time, looking at their surroundings and rubbing their eyes in disbelief as

Headeroonie Bill, Mareekoid, and Augustus appeared before them!

Augustus was the first to speak.

'One is so pleased to see you again, one was so worried that these awfully large woodlice might capture and even kill us. They need to be treated with the greatest respect.'

He then related how the trio had evaded being caught by the narrowest of margins, and how the electric cuckoos had been the greatest of heroes by informing them how close the enemy were.

'One cannot go anywhere near them,' he continued. 'They have erected a village complex near the large lake and have igloo-like buildings that serve as their homes. One cannot ascertain the whereabouts of Mandy and Brutus. They could have been captured, or perhaps they may have escaped. The electric cuckoos may have the answer as they are the only allies we have at the moment to get close to the giant woodlice. Thank goodness you summoned the electric cuckoos when you did; we could have got into all sorts of trouble.'

Headeroonie Bill was the next to speak, assuming his normal bossy role.

'I think it is best to get back to the mansion house and regroup there. It has only been two days but it seems like a week, and the others back home might well be getting worried by now. We need to have all our meetings in secret in case there are spies around, but we also need the input of all our friends.'

After more discussion it was agreed to go back the same way as they had come, in the same two separate groups, not forgetting the two ponies. It was also decided that the ponies should leave first, leaving Augustus behind to go back in the barnmobile. Mareekoid wanted to remain with the ponies because she wanted the chance to collect any recyclable rubbish on the way back that could be converted into something useful.

'If you go on ahead first we will hover above you until we are just out of the reach of the mansion and then land, where Augustus can get out and re-join you. We will then follow slowly behind to make sure you get back alright,' said Tonkas.

'One might have one's own opinion on the matter,' interrupted Augustus, as he felt disgruntled at being ordered around by Tonkas. 'However, this would be a good idea since one is somewhat tired with all this walking around.' He therefore got into the barnmobile alongside Malter and Serendipity.

Headeroonie Bill and Mareekoid got on the ponies and slowly cantered off, The Alisose waited for a safe distance before starting the barnmobile and taking off in a vertical fashion. Soon they reached the predetermined point just out of sight of the mansion house, and again waited until the ponies and their riders caught up.

Headeroonie Bill was the first to speak on the second reunion of the day.

'Glad we caught up again, now it's just one more stage to go and that is to get back to the mansion without any mishap.'

'Yes I realise that,' replied Tonkas. 'I suggest we keep you within sight, but make sure you arrive first and put the ponies away in the stables. Then we will follow behind and also put the barnmobile away in the garage. We will then enter the mansion as separate groups, one group going in the front door and the rest entering via the back. Lastly, we will find our way back into our bedrooms and meet up again sometime after teatime.'

CHAPTER 7

The Rocks Reveal their Secrets

The plan concocted by Tonkas and Headeroonie Bill reached a satisfactory conclusion, everyone sneaking into their own bedrooms undetected by the staff of the mansion house. The barnmobile and ponies had been returned to their respective accommodation and their findings had been secreted away. This led to the question of explaining their absence for a whole night, and the group hoped that their disappearance had gone unnoticed. It was deemed important that any awkward questions were kept to a minimum, and to be very careful of exhibiting any guilty facial expressions. 'Carry on as normal,' was the last comment made by Headeroonie

Bill as they retreated into their own rooms and awaited the signal for supper.

It was not very long before the gong sounded and the kittendogs filtered downstairs individually, starting with Serendipity.

The cook and maid were present in the kitchen and were so engrossed in conversation with each other that they did not notice Serendipity enter. He sat down on his favourite chair around the kitchen table, and was followed by the remaining kittendogs in quick succession, all of them slipping in quietly, not making any sound.

Without warning the cook turned around, having completed her task of washing and drying the previous night's dishes, and only then caught sight of the group awaiting their breakfast.

'Oh, there you are! I didn't see you all yesterday morning when l went to a lot of effort to prepare your favourite morsels. Never mind, it wasn't wasted, though there is still some left over.' She then prepared the food and made no other comments. It would appear that the kittendogs had got away with their little escapade, at least for the time being. Breakfast was consumed without any further conversation and the kittendogs left as quietly as they had come. It was previously agreed that they should all reunite in the largest bedroom that they had, which was Serendipity's, even though he shared it with Malter. As usual, Headeroonie Bill was the first to speak.

'We seem to have been lucky so far in explaining our absence. I have taken the liberty of installing a surveillance system in this room so we know if anyone is approaching. This makes it a good place to have any further meetings because I think there are spies around, but I don't know who they are. We must be very careful of what we say in front of other people. Also, we must build a secret laboratory in the upper floors so we can carry on with our inventions away from the Training Academy, and especially the king. I think he took our refreshment room away so he could keep us away from meeting together, hence the allocation of this room for this purpose. I propose that Tonkas and Mareekoid, who are our chief inventors, report to me. We can use the excuse that we go on litter collecting missions to cover our tracks, and that we are building a recycling plant to produce heat. This will have to be our excuse for being away, when all the time we are doing our best to find Mandy and Brutus.'

The others were relieved when this little speech was over but they all thought it was best to agree with this since they all shared the common objective, "The Quest", as they called it. However, they were bemused when Headeroonie Bill continued with his speech.

'We need to get on with my plan of building a secret laboratory,' he repeated.

Tonkas replied to this, stating that the priority should be the investigation of the writing on the boulder and to a lesser extent the smaller pieces of rock. 'We need to raid the laboratories in the Training Academy to use their special equipment to show the writing better,' he continued. 'After all, we cannot move a massive boulder into the Training Academy.'

'I quite agree,' confirmed Headeroonie Bill. 'A makeshift laboratory would do for the time being until we get things moving.'

'I know of such a place that would make a decent laboratory in the west wing; there are a lot of boarded-up rooms in that area. I discovered this a little time ago, and it would be impossible to get the boulder up several flights of stairs. However, we need a portable special lamp from the Training Academy to take to the boulder itself, preferably the sooner the better before the writing fades. This special lamp detects writing that is invisible to the eye. I read about it in a book,' contributed Tonkas.

This was followed by much chattering of a disorganised nature, and Headeroonie Bill had to bring the commotion and general mayhem to an ending, so that a civilised conclusion could be reached. It was finally agreed that the secret laboratory should proceed, but nothing was more important than the reunion of the kittendogs with Mandy and Brutus. To that end it was decided that indeed the special lamp should be obtained from the Training Academy by fair means or foul. A working party should have a really good look at the boulder and rocks, with Tonkas taking the lead because his special powers of observation which could be used to the best advantage. At the end of the meeting Tonkas and Mareekoid sneaked away from the main group to the place where the boulder was stored.

The back door to the garage was already open when the two siblings reached it, so erring on the side of caution, the pair practically tiptoed their way in and stopped immediately after gaining entry. The new surroundings were very dark, Tonkas and Mareekoid rubbing their eyes until they became accustomed to the difference in light intensity. The only light in the building came from a single window opposite the door from where they stood. Luckily for them there was no one else present.

'Right,' whispered Tonkas. 'Let's find that boulder.'

The pair shuffled carefully around the garage very slowly, looking downwards at the floor periodically to avoid any contact with any obstacles. Their eyes were now becoming more accustomed to the low light levels and they could now distinguish the outline of the barnmobile underneath the tarpaulin. They then knew they were near the boulder, since it was placed underneath the same cover earlier in the day. Tonkas reached in his pocket for the torch he had brought, and said, 'Stay here and keep guard while I look under the cover to have a look around for the boulder.'

Within a short period of time Tonkas had located the object and illuminated the surface with the torch. There were some words scrawled with pencil in a haphazard fashion that must have been written quickly.

Tonkas made out the word "HELP" in block capitals, which was some sort of clue but meant nothing on its own. The word could have been written by anyone at any time and further information was necessary.

Tonkas got out from under the tarpaulin and relayed this information to Mareekoid. 'I had to have a rest because it is hot under all that canvas and my legs have become stiff.'

'Shall I have a go at identifying any writing since I am smaller than you and can squeeze in places you can't?' suggested Mareekoid.

'Good idea,' replied Tonkas. 'I will stay on guard this time while you have a look around.'

Mareekoid did a quick shuffle and entered under the tarpaulin at the same spot where Tonkas had got out, exploring areas that he could not reach. She soon spotted more writing on the boulder even though it was fragmentary. At the rear of the boulder was written "MANDY, BRUTUS" and a date which coincided with the date of the battle. Mareekoid looked around for more information and then found something even more important. In a very small size and written in shaky handwriting was "CAPTURED" and "HELP US."

Mareekoid was overjoyed at this new discovery, and also pleased with herself that she bettered Tonkas on this occasion. She rushed out to tell him; he was rather put out that he didn't have a better look around when he had the chance. However, it was more important to find out about Mandy and Brutus.

Tonkas wanted to confirm Mareekoid's findings so again he entered under the tarpaulin but couldn't find any more information, although he could not get to the areas that his older but smaller sibling could reach. What was the point of struggling with this confined environment, when this information could be obtained if the boulder was moved to a suitable laboratory? *I am the one with special powers and yet Mareekoid turned up trumps.* However, Tonkas had a strange feeling about this large rock and the fact that it had more significance than appeared on the surface. There was nothing for it but to leave the garage and inform the others, so for this reason he got out again from under the tarpaulin.

Mareekoid was still waiting when Tonkas finally extricated himself, and was surprised that she suggested that they return to the mansion, before anyone should turn up unexpectedly. After a brief reconnaissance of the immediate area of the entrance of the building, and the adjacent grounds, the pair scampered to the nearest group of trees to gain cover from any individuals. All the time this was happening, Tonkas could only think of the boulder and the fact that Mareekoid had got the better of him. In his mind he hatched up a plan to re-visit the garage on his own at night and see if he could glean more knowledge. To him the boulder was rather light for its size, but Tonkas was the only one to have noticed this.

Almost as if to distract him, the mansion house reappeared in sight and Tonkas soon put these thoughts to the back of his mind. The pair entered by a seldom-used rear entrance leading to the scullery, and from there they crept upstairs to Serendipity's bedroom and knocked on the door.

'Enter,' a voice boomed from within, and the pair obeyed.

'We have good news,' stated Tonkas, and he related to the assembled kittendogs their new discovery.

'We must gather a working group to rescue Mandy and Brutus,' stated Headeroonie Bill. 'Although on second thoughts it could be unwise to invade their camp, judging by what I saw. It would be better to spy on them in some way, and I think the electric cuckoos can help if they are can be modified in some way. Some improvements could assist them to relay every movement of the giant woodlice, and also their strengths and weaknesses back to us. Hopefully this might minimise the risk to ourselves. The trouble is, we need the necessary parts and knowledge to do this, and also a workshop. It would be really good if we had that secret laboratory to serve as a base to carry out this work.'

It was by now approaching lunch time and soon they would be summoned to the kitchen yet again for another meal, and the worry of being questioned about their activities over the last day or so. Tonkas and Mareekoid wondered why the time had elapsed so quickly, though time goes quickly when you are having fun, it is always said.

Headeroonie Bill then revealed his good news to the kittendogs. 'This morning I met someone from the Training Academy who is willing to help us with our quest. He is called Gregor Nameless who is also editor of the Academy's newspaper, the "Daily Blank". This is known locally as the paper with no news, hence the blank part of the name. Anyway, he knows how to get into the laboratories and help us get supplies to modify the electric cuckoos. They are migratory birds and soon their season here will be over, so they will look conspicuous and will have to be changed into a more suitable bird species.'

Just then, the gong sounded for lunch, at which time all the kittendogs were supposed to be present in the kitchen. Allowances were sometimes made for certain activities such as litter collection and recycling, so perhaps this was why their absence was not questioned very much over the last few days. The kittendogs again filtered down the stairs a few at a time, and were greeted by the cook and maid, Tonkas thinking this was a case of déjà vu. Lunch time passed off well enough, except for the fact that the cook and maid spent a lot of time talking to each other so quietly that the kittendogs could not distinguish the actual topic of their conversation. The only details that were clearly heard were the fact that the kittendogs should be given more useful work to do, and since Mandy and Brutus were no longer present, this meant that there was no effective leadership of the household. The cook and maid had decided between themselves to take charge over their attendance at mealtimes. This was obviously a problem for the kittendogs as it restricted the amount of time they could spend away from the mansion. At the first opportunity they made their excuses to leave the kitchen, and made their way upstairs to their rooms once more, only to reconvene in Serendipity's room to plan the next course of action.

This time it was Serendipity who was the first to speak. 'The cook and that maid are being too bossy with us and are keeping a close eye on us. They could be in cahoots with King. We must make sure we are always around at meal times and perhaps operate a night shift to perform our activities.'

Tonkas saw this as an opportunity to fulfil his plan of going back into the garage for another look at the rocks and so was quick to respond, fabricating a little white lie in the process.

'I would like to volunteer for the first shift because I am the only one who knows where there is some wood to help build the secret laboratory.'

This statement was greeted with a great deal of mumbling by the rest of the kittendogs, which seemed normal for this group of malcontents. Headeroonie Bill was as usual the first to reply.

'It would be of our opinion that you can go ahead with this plan of yours, but you are on your own, except for some of us helping you to get out of the mansion undetected and to assist you with your safe return.'

The rest of the day was passed normally, Mareekoid going about her solitary daily routine of litter collecting, though she finally realised that more emphasis should be placed on accumulating things that could be considered useful to the general cause. The other kittendogs saw this activity as an excuse to gather things which could be used in the construction of the secret laboratory, such as wood and items of ironmongery. Headeroonie Bill spent the time alone investigating the possibility of visiting the Training Academy through accepted means, such as Open Days. He also spent the some of his time on the computer in the library and also the study in the mansion, looking up articles of the Daily Blank newspaper. Tonkas stayed in his bedroom reading books, as this was his favourite hobby, but secretly he was wishing the time away until nightfall when he could execute his plan. There was one obstacle between the present time and the hours of darkness, and that was yet another meal which he could not avoid, since the cook and maid were clamping down on absences. At least evenings were less regimented and the kittendogs could follow their own pursuits, as long as they followed certain guidelines. To Tonkas the wait was interminable and he was much relieved when the gong sounded for the third and final time that day.

The kittendogs wasted no time in going downstairs; many of them were hungry, and they were greeted by the cook, the maid being absent. Again the meal went by with very few comments being made. This was becoming something of a habit since the atmosphere between the cook and kittendogs was becoming somewhat strained. It came as a relief to Tonkas especially, when the meal ended and all returned to their previous locations. The kittendogs were a great deal happier now that they were away from the kitchen, as the tension eased with every step they took up the stairs.

'Things were so much better when Mandy and Brutus were here. They looked after us so well,' moaned Serendipity when the group reassembled in his bedroom. 'The cook has become so unfriendly recently and she spends so much time staring at us. The sooner our parents are back with us the better, so that things can get back to normal.'

The kittendogs nodded in agreement, with Augustus adding, 'One must have a plan on how to find Mandy and Brutus and one must put this into effect as soon as possible. One will assist Tonkas with his idea if no one else has a better one.'

'I wish you would not use the word "one" quite so many times in quick succession. I do not understand you at times,' replied Tonkas.

'Any help at all would exceedingly useful,' commented Malter. Tonkas thought that he would avoid any of this so-called assistance, and escape by himself during the hours of darkness. He turned on his heels and made his way to his bedroom where he could cogitate and contemplate on his own. What course of action he should consider? Lying on his bed thinking to himself, he fell asleep with boredom.

*

He awoke with a start and turned his head to the window and noticed that it was now dark. It was time to put his plan into action. Quickly dressing in dark clothes, he equipped himself with a torch and a few small hand tools in case he needed them to gain entry into the garage. As quietly as he could, Tonkas opened the bedroom door and crept downstairs to the seldom-used door, which although locked was quickly picked. The conditions were favourable: the ground was dry, a full moon casting some light to the otherwise dimly lit surroundings. Tonkas scampered towards the undergrowth where he could not be detected. Under the shelter of a tree he stopped to get his breath back and to pause for a while, looking back at the house to check whether any other kittendogs had followed him. He could not believe his good fortune in that his plan had so far succeeded without any interference. Satisfied that the coast was clear, he continued towards the garage. Although the path was dark, and made somewhat spooky by the tall trees and shrubs, the way forward was relatively easy due to the moonlight. The garage was soon reached, and although this was the long way round from the mansion house, it was safer, affording cover in case someone was watching. *Better err on the side of caution*, thought Tonkas, as he gained entry to the building through the same door as before, which was still surprisingly unlocked from the previous visit. Tonkas collapsed on the floor as soon as he got inside with all his exertions, and felt like dozing off to sleep.

However, he realised that this was a risky thing to do as there might be a chance he could be found the next morning still inside the garage.

'Hello,' said a voice from behind a pile of straw, and a shadowy figure appeared. It was Malter!

'How on earth did you get here before me? I took every possible precaution, and furthermore, how did you know I was going to come here?'

'It's your fault for talking in your sleep,' answered Malter. 'I heard everything you said. Luckily for you, no one else was around.'

Tonkas was rather discontented at being foiled once again. 'First Mareekoid and now you. Why can't I have more privacy? Oh well, now that you are here you can help me move the boulder so I can get confirm what Mareekoid found.'

The pair of them moved the boulder enough for Tonkas to gain access to the back and indeed confirm the scribbled writing. In frustration, he gave the boulder a smack with his paw-like right hand and a very strange thing happened. A small area of the boulder flicked open and then fell off as though it was released by a spring. The gap was large enough for Tonkas to get his whole arm inside and as he did so the whole boulder fell apart like two halves of an Easter egg.

There was a clatter as the contents spilled out on to the garage floor, revealing partly constructed electric cuckoos, numerous pieces of electrical items, and an envelope with more writing on the cover. This said, "From Mandy and Brutus, to our children. To be opened as soon as possible if anything should happen to us."

This is strange, Tonkas though. *Did Mandy and Brutus know in advance they were going to disappear? How and why did this rock get to the battle site unless our parents took it there?* Tonkas opened the envelope and removed several sheets of paper, which were plans on how to manufacture and modify the electric cuckoos. This was a very opportune time to discover these plans, as the cuckoos would have to be modified if they were to have any use. The night that the group spent out of doors proved how useful they could be when functioning properly.

Just then, Malter re-appeared, torch in hand, to enquire if there was any progress. The sight of the boulder, now left in pieces, answered the question without the need for any reply.

'In that case why don't we see if there are any clues contained in the small bits of rock?' he suggested. Tonkas felt he could not disagree and the two of them started on the task of bagging the pieces of rock fragment.

'Wait a minute. Someone should be on guard duty outside the garage, in case anyone hears anything from the house or anywhere else,' said Tonkas.

'Soon we will be singing the anyway song if any more anys are spoken,' replied Malter, and the pair rolled about with laughter on the garage floor. When they had finished frolicking about they whispered the anyway song, which went:

Anyway, anyway anyway any, anywhere, anytime, anyplace, anyhow, anyone…

The phrase was repeated a second time and then a

strange thing happened. The rock fragments shattered all on their own, revealing the contents of more electrical items and parts of prefabricated artificial birds.

'I must remember this when I next need to open a tin of beans without a ring pull,' said Malter. 'There must be something magical about that little song. It may come in useful sometime.'

'Just like the barnpotting song,' replied Tonkas, who then added that it was now a good time to tidy up all the rock fragments. The next task was to remove the parts to the mansion, to serve as evidence to the others. A sack was conveniently lying close by, just large enough to hold all the pieces, and the all-important envelope containing assembly instructions. Enough straw and other packing material was around to prevent the discovery rattling around in the sack.

'Come on, it's time to go before it gets light again. We must get back indoors, and hide all this stuff. There are some loose floorboards by that back door of the mansion. We can put it there for the time being and then retire for the night so we can wake up refreshed in the morning. What a strange and rewarding expedition this has been, provided we get back without any mishap,' noted Tonkas.

The lucky duo made their way out of the garage with their spoils and regained the warmth and safety of the mansion, unseen by anyone except the wildlife. The findings were indeed hidden under the floorboards successfully and the pair found the comfort of their own beds.

CHAPTER 8

The Electric Cuckoos Are Modified

and the King Gets a Reward

The sun was shining brightly through Tonkas's bedroom window as he woke up to the sound of knocking on the door. Malter entered without waiting for any reply to his agitated attempts at waking the occupant.

'Come on, you have overslept and it's getting late. I have told the others about what happened last night and they want to see you before breakfast to hear the facts from you. I will give you five minutes to get dressed and then join us in Serendipity's room. Now hurry up.'

Malter left quickly and shut the door behind him to give Tonkas some privacy. Luckily there was a tap and basin in every bedroom and Tonkas used this to freshen up. Having dressed, he opened the door very quietly, and crept along the corridor to the appointed room, where there was a great deal of commotion going on. With a previously agreed knock, Tonkas entered to a chorus of cheers and back slapping.

'Well done,' bellowed Headeroonie Bill. 'This is the breakthrough we needed. Now we must secure all these artefacts properly where we can work on them in peace and quiet. We will use the tools and spare parts you found last night to alter the electric cuckoos. The bosses at the Training Academy are having one of their self-congratulatory days where I have heard that the king has been awarded the Werdna Prize for Tact and Diplomacy.'

The Alisose replied, 'That means that all the staff will be out of the way and we can move all our acquisitions to the west wing, where our new secret laboratory is going to be built. I think the king will be awarding the prize to himself as no one else would do it, at least none of us.'

'While he is away we could start the modifications to the electric cuckoos, and also start building the laboratory. Arrangements for sleeping quarters could be started so we can devise a shift pattern,' continued Headeroonie Bill.

'Don't forget to keep the door as it is, complete with cobwebs and all that dust and dirt. That way it looks as though the place has been abandoned. Not only that, I insist on being in charge of the construction of sense of direction glands,' added The Alisose.

The others reluctantly agreed, taking into consideration that her powers of persuasion would eventually win over any opposition. 'Better to give in now than risk a long and drawn out war of attrition,' was one comment muttered by an unidentified voice. Another opinion was that The Alisose is incapable of finding her way around the Luniverse, so how could she be capable of improving such a navigational device, especially if was made from matchsticks like the prototype?

'I would prefer Mickel to give you some help in this matter,' concluded Headeroonie Bill. That was the end of the debate and general excitement, as the gong sounded for breakfast. An air of gloom and despondency descended amongst them when they entered the kitchen, only to find the king there, equipped with all the paraphernalia associated with his position of high office.

'I wish I could make myself invisible,' whispered Mickel to Serendipity, 'because this can only be bad news. I either want to hide behind a pillar or under a cupboard so I that I don't see him.'

However, the tension was lifted when it was revealed that the king was to attend a course at a Lunversity, and give a keynote speech on "How to Win Friends and Influence People" to other inventors. He was to be away for several days and the cook and maid were to accompany him in the chauffer-driven luxury car. The kittendogs were to look after themselves, except for the occasional checks by security staff at prescribed intervals.

The kittendogs could hardly contain their excitement at the thought of all this freedom from the atmosphere of tyranny and repression.

The cook and maid were very friendly for a change and everyone was very happy. Breakfast was over very quickly, the king departing very soon after his short speech, taking his two obedient servants with him. This left the kittendogs alone. As soon as they were gone Headeroonie Bill suggested that they should reconvene in the usual place after all the clearing away was done.

Headeroonie Bill wished to reopen the debate but was interrupted by the general excitement. He tried to state that he would contact Gregor Nameless and establish links with the inventors in the Training Academy. Apart from The Alisose and Mickel, the rest of the group elected themselves to continue with the construction of the secret laboratory, which was to include a kitchen. Mareekoid, however, wished to go out on her own, scavenging for materials including pig feathers for the modifications to the electric cuckoos.

The group made their way downstairs to the kitchen once more, after collecting rucksacks and bags to accommodate belongings necessary for the day. Sandwiches were prepared, and they all left the house towards the village, armed with a plethora of builder's tools and a wheelbarrow. Outside one of the shops Headeroonie Bill saw a familiar face who he recognised at once. It was Gregor Nameless, who by chance was heading in the direction of the mansion house. Headeroonie Bill did the introductions. It was conveyed to Gregor that the kittendogs could do whatever they wished for the next few days, so it was suggested that they all went back to the Training Academy. The reason, Gregor explained, was that the inventors of the Training Academy were very sympathetic to the plight of the kittendogs, with respect to the disappearance of Mandy and Brutus, and the somewhat oppressive atmosphere prevalent in the mansion house, which had been explained to them by Gregor.

'Why don't you come back to our laboratories?' said Gregor. 'Nearly all our people are away at the conference that the king is attending. There is only a few staff left and they will welcome you with open arms. Miss Jet Drawls is the chief and her understudy is Anita Moontogs, and they are willing to help you in any way they can. I was on my way to tell you.'

As expected, the kittendogs were delighted to hear this news, and Tonkas in particular was amazed at all the good luck they were having.

This revelation was the followed by a cacophony of cheering and arm waving amongst the kittendogs. Afterwards it was agreed that the original plan of collecting building materials was to be abandoned. However there still remained the problem of where to store the fragments of electric cuckoos so carefully obtained the previous night.

The many characters made a spectacular sight as they merrily marched along the narrow pavement of the main village street, sometimes wandering into the road to the dismay and annoyance of passing motorists. The sight of a wheelbarrow in which The Alisose sat, complete with an axe and chainsaw, concerned many a pedestrian and shopkeeper alike. To their great relief a country lane soon appeared and this was used as means of access to the Training Academy, and Gregor thought that stealth was the better approach. A shed stood in the corner of a field which was used by the Training Academy for storage, so the addition of a few more items made little difference. The kittendogs were very pleased to relieve themselves of the heavy equipment, for now much more care was required to avoid being caught by security personnel employed by the Academy. The greater concern was to get inside the laboratories unnoticed by anyone except friends.

Again they were lucky in that the path to the Training Academy was sheltered by a tall hedge, although the other side of the path was bordered by an open field. No one else was around to observe their progress. Soon the tradesmen's entrance to the laboratories was gained, and Anita Moontogs was there to greet them.

'Hello and welcome. Do come and have around and have a look at our facilities. We will do whatever we can to help you build your own laboratory. Gregor has informed me of your predicament, and to help you we have experience in the matter of surveillance devices. Please follow me upstairs. You will be safe there.'

The kittendogs needed no further encouragement and followed Anita as they quickly reached the reception room which was manned by Miss Jet Drawls. She welcomed them in a similar fashion.

'Do follow me to our canteen where you can have your lunch and recover from that long walk of yours.

After that we can discuss your plans. I am sure we can assist, we have the same common enemy in the king and we like the prospect of getting revenge.'

'Yes,' interrupted Mickel. 'I was hurt both mentally and physically by flying fragments of dirty tricks in the battle of the mansion and the giant killer woodlice.'

After lunch, Anita showed the kittendogs the store of wood and other building materials in the Department of Constructions, and all the multifarious workshops where all sorts of engineering work was undertaken. This included the electronics area which could reconfigure the essential parts to alter the electric cuckoos into a more suitable bird. This procedure was named by Anita as Operation Pigeoncat. The concern was that the energy required for these devices to maintain their duration of flight was greater than the mechanical birds already possessed. Augustus suggested that they could use a false eye as a miniature solar panel to provide extra energy; at least this was a theory. The Alisose mentioned that it was she who developed the sense of direction gland, which could be used as a control panel.

'This is exceedingly wonderful news,' said Headeroonie Bill. 'I think we could have everything we need to put Operation Pigeoncat into effect, and perhaps your spare building materials could go a long way to construct our secret laboratory.'

'All these things are very good,' said Gregor, appearing on the scene rather suddenly, having previously slipped off unnoticed to attend to his newspaper duties. 'It's very convenient that the Training Academy is closed due to the ceremonies elsewhere. I suggest that enough material is removed to start the process of building the laboratory, but not such a great amount that will be noticed as missing. We can get some to the mansion house using the Training Academy van and collect your tools left in the shed on the way. After that, collect all the pieces of electric cuckoo you have removed from the garage and place them in the area set aside for your laboratory.'

Headeroonie Bill was not pleased with Gregor taking control over proceedings, but nevertheless kept quiet on this occasion. Instead The Alisose and Tonkas were the first of the kittendogs to reply, and the rest followed in agreement with the normal babble and confusion. In the absence of an alternative plan it made sense to proceed, despite the fact that Anita, Jet, and Gregor were entirely unknown to all the kittendogs except Headeroonie Bill. Without any further ado, the entire group of characters made their way out of the building to where the Training Academy vehicles were kept.

Anita drove a van to the rear of the workshops while all the others walked the short distance. When they got there Anita had already started to select some oddments of wood and plumbing materials from a skip covered by a tarpaulin and ready to be transported away for recycling.

'This will not be missed because no one will check the contents before it is removed. I will keep an eye on things, and see if anything more turns up. There is not enough room for all of you to come with me, so some of you should stay behind and discuss what you want to do regarding Operation Pigeoncat.'

'I wish to remain behind along with Tonkas, who has special powers which could help with this project,' said Headeroonie Bill. 'I think The Alisose should also come with us because she is in charge of the sense of direction glands, and Sylvate should go with you since she sleeps and snores a lot. Malter knows where the pieces of electric cuckoos are hidden. Mareekoid is still looking for pig feathers. This leaves Augustus, Serendipity, and Mickel left.' Turning in their direction, he said, 'So what do you want to do?'

'One would certainly like to decide what to do oneself. After all, when the rat is away the kittendogs should play,' said Augustus, referring to the king. 'I think one ought to collect the wheelbarrow, chainsaw, and hatchet from the shed and return them to where they came from. It was a pointless exercise bringing them unless a use can be made for them on the way back. Perhaps Serendipity and Mickel can help me do this.'

Serendipity needed no further encouragement, volunteering straight away, adding that he had spotted some felled trees that could be sawn into shorter lengths. He added that the lengths could be used as uprights for benching either for the secret laboratory or else outdoors. The inclusion of the chainsaw and hatchet would then not be a pointless exercise after all.

It was therefore concluded that indeed this would be the best course of action to take, so the pair of them enthusiastically jumped in the van alongside Anita.

As soon as the van was loaded with the materials and personnel, Anita carefully drove away. She made sure that there was enough room in the back to accommodate the tools with some room to spare for other oddments that might be collected on the way. In next to no time the entrance to the lane was reached, adjacent to the shed belonging to the Training Academy. There happened to be a layby in which the van could stay a while. The kittendogs got out and scampered along the track as before to retrieve the tools for succeeding in the mission.

Anita continued the journey, stopping in a short while to let Serendipity and Mickel gather some wood with the tools and wheelbarrow. They were to reunite at the mansion house in the evening. Augustus glanced out of the back window and noticed Malter trying his best to catch up with them.

'I nearly forgot about our friend. He is the only one that knows where the pieces of electric cuckoo are hidden, now that Tonkas has stayed behind.'

'Yes, that's right; I will wait until he arrives. There is room for him in the van now,' answered Anita.

Malter arrived, who was out of breath and unable to speak. He clambered into the back of the van, positioning his arms and legs somewhat uncomfortably on piles of wood, tools, and the handles of the wheelbarrow. Closing the rear door, he beckoned to Anita to recommence the journey to the intended destination. This was achieved in a matter of minutes, Malter opening the rear door of the van and collapsing in a heap on the ground as the vehicle screeched to a halt. All this happened to the rear of the mansion house, very close to the rear door of secretiveness.

'Oh good,' Malter huffed. 'We are very close to the

loose floorboards where the bits of mechanical birds are. Let's retrieve them right away while the coast is clear and get them upstairs.'

Augustus extricated himself from the front of the van so that Anita could park the van in a safe manner before getting out herself, and walking to the rear door of the mansion. After helping Malter find his feet, she then proceeded to remove the tools and then the wood with other items of ironmongery.

Malter, finding the energy to move, made his way to the rear entrance door and then to the secret hiding place inside the mansion. The artefacts were quickly retrieved and shown to Anita, who was delighted to see them.

'I have seen something like this before, although these particular objects appear to be broken. We tried many years ago to manufacture radio-controlled birds for our research studies, but they were not realistic enough and not very durable. These look a much better design even though this type of bird is now out of season for the time of year. Where did you get them from?'

'Well, these were found inside false rocks left at the battle area with instructions for modifications. They were first invented by Mareekoid, who is not here for the moment. What we have here are slightly different to the prototype and must have been worked on by Mandy and Brutus before they disappeared. Why they were left by the giant killer woodlice is beyond me. Being concealed inside rocks must have prevented the enemy from seeing them.'

'Well these are too important a find to leave lying

around. They should come back with me to the Training Academy to be studied further. It would be good to compare them with the electric cuckoos, but perhaps they have flown back to their own country. Perhaps your Mareekoid would know. Don't worry about security. Apart from the two of us the premises are deserted, as is your mansion house.'

Just then Augustus came running up to Anita to inform her that the van had been unloaded, and enquired what to do with the contents.

'Show me where your secret laboratory is going to be and bring some of the wood with you. I will help you and bring some of the plumbing.'

'What about the bits of electric cuckoos?' asked Malter.

'Don't worry,' replied Augustus. 'One had a dream last night. It started with the word "Mana", and then one realised that Brutus was trying to communicate with us by using that phrase. One was given the impression that the both the Training Academy and mansion house will be devoid of enemies and spies, and we can do anything we like for a time. One thinks that Brutus is looking after us somehow, and this is why we are having this unbelievable run of good luck. One also thinks that perhaps the word was Mana which is a foreign word for power, effectiveness, prestige, and power. Mana also has a supernatural undertone.'

Malter added that he thought Brutus had somehow contrived the removal of all the staff from both the Training Academy and the mansion house by brainwashing them using his special word, Mana.

Brutus called the people at the Training Academy infidels, at least the people who did not comply with his plans. Malter also thought that Brutus had special powers, but since he was captured he could not use them to the greatest magnitude, and that Tonkas was first in line to inherit them in times of need.

'Never mind all that, let's get on with the job in hand,' said Anita, who by now was getting impatient with this diversion. 'Now show me where the west wing is and put the bits of electric cuckoo in this cardboard box I have brought with me.'

Malter, afraid of offending Anita, did he was bid, and showed her along corridors that were seldom used to the rear of the main building. This was followed by another corridor which led to the west wing, which was disused except for storage, until the area designated as the secret laboratory was reached. At this point the two of them were becoming very tired with the weight of their burden, and were only too glad to rest for a while. All that they were carrying was deposited on the floor outside the door to the secret laboratory. It was still encased in cobwebs and dust through years of neglect. Entry was gained with a gentle shove of Anita's shoulder, though it was some time before their eyes adjusted to the dark conditions. As soon as it was possible, the group cautiously shuffled towards the windows, and with a great deal of effort managed to open some of them. It was a great sense of relief to obtain some fresh air, and to be rid of the musty atmosphere. However, it would be some time before a complete exchange of air could be achieved.

'At least you have swept the floor beforehand,'

noted Anita. 'With the windows open we have more light so that we can see what we are doing. We ought to bring in the building materials from outside so a start can be made to build your laboratory.'

This was duly accomplished with the items stacked tidily in one corner of the room, and a reconnaissance mission undertaken to ascertain the condition of the plumbing and electrics. Again, luck was on their side when it was discovered that everything was in working order, so a start could be made on the actual building, albeit on a small scale. There were enough materials to make a complete length of benching together with a sink, but not enough expertise available at the present time to perform this operation. For some reason Malter decided to look out of the window and by chance saw Augustus and Serendipity outside with some tools and a wheelbarrow. There was no wood, however; perhaps they may have left that behind, having too much to carry.

'Why are you looking out of the window?' asked Anita, and Mickel relayed the latest information of the sighting.

'Oh good, do they know their way up here?'

Mickel nodded in an affirmative manner, but still suggested that he leave the room and bring them to the secret laboratory, to which Anita conveyed her agreement. Some time elapsed, however, before the two kittendogs returned, and in the intervening time Anita made a start on the first bench, alongside the windows, where there happened to be a water supply and tap. There was an indication of a sink had once been in position, judging by the marks on the wall and disused pipes lying on the floor. The size of the room and marks on the floorboards gave an impression that there may have been bunk beds, or perhaps even a dormitory in the past. There also was an anteroom which Anita thought could be used as a secret refreshment room.

Anita's thoughts were diverted by the arrival of Serendipity, Mickel, and Augustus. Mareekoid then entered, who explained that she could not find any pig feathers. She had to abandon her search, and had to make do with a bag full of assorted bird feathers. Anita had a wry smile on her face that she did not show to the rest of them. *Someone's idea of a practical joke*, she thought.

'Well, now that you are back, give me a hand with this benching. I cannot complete this by myself because it is too heavy. I wish that I could be like an octopus and have plenty of arms and legs.'

The kittendogs could not wait to offer their assistance since it had been a long-term objective to have this facility. It just so happened that the materials Anita had brought were carefully removed from a previous refurbishment at the Training Academy. Since everything was prefabricated it was just a matter of reassembling them. 'They make everything easy these days by making everything look like some sort of kit,' said Anita. 'All you have to do is put it back in the reverse order that it was taken apart. Start with the legs which are made of metal, and then bolt the parts together with the front and back rails. Next, bolt on the back and sides followed lastly by the top, just like a table.'

The kittendogs did exactly that and moved the completed assemblage towards the window. This was repeated two more times, and so provided a length of benching along the entire wall with enough room for the missing sink at the end. Next to follow were some drawer units and the job was finished.

'This is absolutely wonderful,' observed Serendipity. 'This is just want we have wanted for a very long time.'

However, it was now getting dark and Anita thought they should go back to the Training Academy where they could reunite with all the kittendogs and catch up on the events of the day.

'Collect all you need. You are welcome to stay with us in our student dormitories for as long as you need, and don't forget the box of electric cuckoo parts. We can work on them at the laboratories and see how The Alisose is getting on with the sense of direction glands.'

The five kittendogs reluctantly left the room and accompanied Anita out of the mansion house and to the van.

'One needs to know if there is room in the van for all of us, or does one have to walk back to the Training Academy?' asked Augustus.

'Of course there is room for all of you. There is plenty of space now that the back of the van has been emptied,' answered Anita. 'Now let's get back, I am sure we are all tired and need to eat.'

Serendipity made sure that he had the box of electric cuckoo parts, and was the first to get into the van, placing the precious cargo on the floor of the passenger seat. The others were soon to follow, even though some had to sit in the back of the vehicle. At least there was more room now that the materials were taken away. Anita seemed to be in a hurry, driving somewhat erratically, and rather fast on the narrow roads. She explained that she had forgotten her keys and was afraid there was no one left in the Training Academy to let them in. Malter put her mind at rest when he stated that he had picked them up earlier from the pile of plumbing.

Anita mumbled to herself ungraciously, 'Wish you told me that earlier,' leaving Malter embarrassed.

Anita then relaxed, knowing the keys were safe, and drove more carefully until the Training Academy laboratories were reached.

In the loading bay there was a welcoming party made up of the rest of the kittendogs and Gregor.

'Good news. I have made progress with the sense of direction glands and have made several of them of different sizes, all black, spherical, and shiny with a screw attachment for ease of installation,' roared The Alisose excitedly.

The kittendogs were most excited by this news, Serendipity stating that this had been a most useful and constructive day. However, it was getting late and there was still a lot to do. Arrangements had been made for the kittendogs to remain in dormitories overnight at least, or possibly longer, provided the infidels stayed away from the Training Academy.

The whole party made their way to the infidel canteen where they were greeted by Jet Drawls, who had been busy all day preparing a vast meal to celebrate the recent achievements.

The atmosphere was very jovial and The Alisose was the happiest of the group, especially now that the pieces of electric cuckoos had been delivered along with a collection of feathers. The Alisose wanted to work on the cuckoos straight away but was dismayed to learn that Anita and Jet were to resume the following day with Operation Pigeoncat.

The evening passed all too quickly, hilarity and partying being the order of the night, taking advantage of the absence of infidels. When it was over the kittendogs were shown to the dormitory and in no time at all they were all fast asleep, even Sylvate, who was snoring loudly the whole night long.

*

Tonkas woke the next morning to the sound of the remaining electric cuckoos, which had decided to return to their masters. It would seem that they were bored with their freedom and wished to return to the place of peace and quiet ready to be adapted in the cause of a greater need.

Just then, Headeroonie Bill woke up, also hearing the sound of the electric cuckoos, mumbling in a drowsy condition that he must have summoned them unknowingly.

'Get them in here by opening the window and I'll capture them.'

Tonkas obeyed just as the mechanical devices reached what would have been glass. One after the other they crashed onto the floor and passed out, but not before there was a cacophony of squeaks and squawks. The noise woke the rest of the kittendogs as Tonkas pounced and collected them in one swift move.

'Good work! Now we can start working on them and convert our friends into pigeoncats using the plans you found in the hollow rock. Good job I had my calling whistle with me, they may have flown away forever,' said Headeroonie Bill.

'Not before we have had some food, I am so hungry after all the exertions of yesterday,' replied Tonkas.

The rest of the kittendogs had by now arisen, with some of them dressed though still in a sleepy state. There was then a knock on the door and Anita said, 'What is all this noise about? I thought I heard something like birds being throttled, may I come in?'

Tonkas was the first to open the door and told Anita about the captured electric cuckoos.

Anita was delighted to hear this news. 'This means we can manufacture more pigeoncats, but I suggest we do this after breakfast.'

The kittendogs needed no second bidding and followed Anita to the infidel canteen where a hearty full English breakfast was waiting for them. There was much excitement around the many tables, and the atmosphere was so much better than at the mansion house. Both Gregor and Jet were present and everyone was very happy. There was disappointment in the offing however, when it was realised that there were many chores to be completed before the more rewarding work of pigeoncat construction could be undertaken. The clearing away of dishes and the washing of the dishes was an activity no one looked forward to, especially Mareekoid, who ran away as fast as she could. Luckily there were others who were more willing to help and the task was completed in good time.

Anita and Jet then called a meeting with the kittendogs most involved with Operation Pigeoncat, this of course including The Alisose, Headeroonie Bill, and Tonkas.

Malter then spoke of being afraid of being omitted from future activities.

'What about the role that I played? After all, it was with my help that the recovery of the electric cuckoos from the garage and the subsequent concealment took place. The cook and maid might have found the pieces if it wasn't for me.'

'Yes of course,' replied Headeroonie Bill. 'It is only right that you should help. We need to consult the paperwork that was found at the same time.'

Anita agreed with this and was very sympathetic towards Malter's request. Both Tonkas and Malter were instrumental in discovering the electric cuckoo parts together with the all-important instructions. With the short meeting concluded, the attendees were in total agreement on how to proceed. The first course of action was to resume the activity where the materials were stored and work from there.

'We ought to collect the electric cuckoos you have just acquired,' added Anita. 'Bring everything you have and combine it all together in the laboratory.'

This plan was duly carried out with a great deal of care. A number of boxes were needed to house the neutralised birds, wrapping them in such a manner that little or no damage would be incurred. The four characters then conveyed the precious cargo to the Training Academy laboratories, which was devoid of any infidels. It was due to Brutus's power of hypnotism via the special word, Mana. By using this word, all the infidels were now attending the combined Training Academy and Mansion House Self-Congratulatory Convention for the foreseeable future. Only Tonkas knew this for certain, but did not wish to tell the others. Nevertheless, Tonkas wished that Operation Pigeoncat would go ahead as quickly as possible because there was no telling how long this spell of Brutus could be sustained. The kittendogs' secret laboratories were not completed yet, although at least start had been made.

All these thoughts were going through Tonkas's mind as the group made their way to the Training Academy laboratories for the first phase of reconstruction of the mechanical birds.

The Alisose collected the sense of direction glands she prepared the previous day and assembled them into the electric cuckoos as described on the instructions found in the hollow rock found at the battle. Next she removed the false eyes and replaced them with the solar energy eyes also found in the hollow rock. This would enable the electric cuckoos to fly for a greater length of time.

Just then Serendipity appeared, joining The Alisose on the production team. Her job was to implant the electrical devices to relay photographic evidence back to a central reconnaissance laboratory. For the time being this was to be located in the Training Academy laboratories, but the long-term plan was to house the equipment in the secret laboratory in the mansion house.

The final stage was to apply the feathers to the outside of the mechanical birds to give them a more realistic appearance. The electric cuckoos were thus transmogrified into pigeoncats in order to provide evidence of the giant killer woodlice encampment. The real problem was how to overcome the enemy with so few resources; one needed to know the strengths and weaknesses of the woodlice.

Enough of the pigeoncats were therefore completed to perform a reconnaissance mission that very afternoon, following a short test flight. Headeroonie Bill wished to be responsible for this action after lunch: the time had passed by very quickly in the morning session.

Both Anita and Jet made an entrance into the laboratory at that moment and had to drag the kittendogs away from their work. She stated that lunch was ready prepared by Gregor and a few of the kittendogs who volunteered to provide a change of diet.

'Come on you lot. It's time to down tools and have something to eat. Besides, there are enough completed pigeoncats for a trial run this afternoon,' said Anita.

Serendipity and The Alisose were the first to leave the laboratory; they had done the bulk of the work and felt justified to put their tools away. Malter and Mareekoid seemed to be content with sorting and applying the feathers to give the mechanical birds a more realistic appearance.

All the kittendogs were ready for the meal, and even willing to help with the clearing up, such was their enthusiasm to see the new pigeoncats on a surveillance mission. Even more important were the possible results that could be obtained and the latest news of Mandy and Brutus.

The washing, drying, and clearing away was completed in record time as no one wanted to be left out of the launch of the new pigeoncats. The venue of this ground-breaking event was to be at the front lawn of the main Training Academy building and was to be initiated by Headeroonie Bill.

At the appointed time and place, everyone congregated. The atmosphere was strained with the tension as the best two pigeoncats were prepared with the greatest care. Headeroonie Bill activated the on/off switch, set the destination co-ordinates on the sense of direction gland, and placed them on the nearest branch. With a quick blast of the whistle the birds were on their way and all anyone could do was wait.

'Well, let's go to the laboratory and see how the pigeoncats are progressing. A tracker device has been included – Jet installed it when you weren't looking. This was something that you overlooked, otherwise you could not ascertain their whereabouts,' said Anita.

'Oh dear,' replied Tonkas. 'Good job you thought of that, I was thinking that we could receive images and that would do, but it is better to know exactly where they are at all times.'

Anita and Tonkas were the first to reach the instruments capable of providing the position of the pigeoncats. There was an audible beep on a screen indicating their whereabouts, which happened to be close to the giant killer woodlice encampment. The beep then stopped, indicating that the pigeoncats had stopped moving. Anita and Tonkas's attention was turned towards several flashing monitors with indistinct images. Suddenly these images became clearer as outlines of igloo-like structures appeared.

'Is there any chance of getting inside any of these igloos or at least acquiring more information of this encampment? Or is this too risky?' asked Tonkas.

'Try getting the pigeoncats to fly around the area a little more,' replied Anita.

'I don't know how to do that,' said Headeroonie Bill.

'I can command them with my special whistle, but it is too dangerous to get them inside the igloos even if it is possible. As yet, I do not have the expertise to control the fine details. All I can do for now is enable the pigeoncats to circle around the encampment to see what they can discover, and then get them to return as soon as possible. Don't forget this is only a test run.'

'Yes, alright,' replied Tonkas. 'It is better not to risk the pigeoncats after all the work we have gone through in making them. Let's see if we can get some results though.'

Many of the group gathered around the monitors with bated breath. Preference to the seating closest to the monitors was given to the creators of the flying devices, although Anita who had given so much of her time, and Jet who had provided the facilities, still managed to acquire the best chairs. The images were in black and white and rather blurred due to second-hand parts being used. Enough detail was evident, however, to ascertain the shape and size of the igloo houses and the grotesque form of the woodlice which looked nothing like the original creatures.

After a while there appeared two familiar figures that seemed to be engaged in the menial task of collecting water from a river and pouring it into a large trough outside the largest of the igloos. Both Tonkas and Headeroonie Bill nearly fell off their stools with both shock and excitement. They were Mandy and Brutus!

The group were very excited at seeing them after all this time, both Mandy and Brutus looked well, if unkempt in appearance. They were closely guarded by woodlice so there was no chance of them escaping from the fortress.

'What can we do to help them?' wailed The Alisose.

'There is nothing we can do for the time being,' answered Headeroonie Bill. 'It is rather late in the day to do much. I think I ought to get the pigeoncats back while there is some daylight, and think about the situation overnight.'

'We need a plan,' said Mickel.

'First of all, I am going to recall the pigeoncats to make sure they get back safely. They can be used another time,' said Headeroonie Bill.

'I will go outside until they arrive; the rest of you can stay here if you like,' commented Tonkas. 'Perhaps the other creators could come as well.'

Only The Alisose agreed, so the two left the building and waited on the lawn from where the pigeoncats were first launched. Headeroonie Bill then gave a blast on his whistle to summon the mechanical birds. The wait was a short one as the silence of the night air was broken by the noise of wings fluttering, followed by the birds themselves. *Another successful night,* thought Tonkas as he caught a glimpse of Anita rushing down the steps from the Training Academy front entrance to the lawn.

Anita was breathless as she rushed over to them. 'You know the bunch of keys that Malter handed to me the other day? Well on the bunch was a key I didn't recognise and I don't know how it got there. Anyway, we have a door that is always locked in the laboratories so I thought I would try the key in it. Much to my surprise it fitted, so naturally I went in the room. Now I wish I hadn't because I had the shock of my life. The place was full of those giant woodlice in tanks and they were being fed by some sort of liquid. You must help me check this over, and decide what to do as soon as possible.'

CHAPTER 9

An Awful Discovery

Anita, Tonkas, and The Alisose discussed what to do next. Was it better to try and deal with this problem at once or wait until the morning? Furthermore, do they keep this revelation to themselves or do they tell the others?

The three of them contemplated their options on the short walk back to the main entrance to the Training Academy, eventually deciding to have a quick look around the hidden laboratory to assess the situation. The problem was, who was responsible for this hideous creation and to what purpose? Considering all the risks involved it was deemed that the greatest care should be exercised at all times.

Anita was the first to enter the evil-smelling den of decadence, turning the key in the lock so the noise was kept to an absolute minimum.

The interior was even gloomier than the secret laboratory, although it seemed relatively quiet. Tonkas and The Alisose were ushered in and the door closed behind them, and again their eyes took a while to adjust to the darkness. Anita had already paid a visit to this Manipulations Laboratory so she was aware of the immediate surroundings. Despite all this the trio held their breath in awe of what might happen to them. Gradually, their eyes became accustomed to the conditions, as they resisted the temptation to switch on the lights to avoid suspicion. There was enough light being emitted from the tanks to move around and to familiarise themselves with the surroundings. Now it was more obvious to the group what was going on.

Tonkas was the first to say anything, and even then it was in a hushed voice. 'These tanks must be a breeding ground for these horrible creatures that captured Mandy and Brutus. Is there a way of destroying this equipment and the killer woodlice at the same time? Then perhaps it could reduce the numbers at the encampment.'

'You are implying that somehow these woodlice either escape on their own or someone else helps them on their way,' suggested Anita.

'Look, there is some handwriting on the labels for each of the tanks and I recognise who it belongs to. The king is responsible for all this, and this is where he lives up to his name. He is manipulating the once friendly woodlice into fiendish ones, which are against us in every way,' said The Alisose.

'I suspect the cook and maid have something to do with this as well. It could explain their aggressive behaviour towards us. Remember all the strange awkward glances, the whispered conversations and bossiness in the kitchen,' continued Tonkas.

'The trouble is, what we do now? If we kill the woodlice they will smell in time,' interrupted The Alisose. 'I think we need to starve them so they die gradually and then inject them with preservative so they look normal to any outsider. Perhaps we can clog the drip feed to deprive them of nourishment overnight and see what happens.'

Anita nodded her consent. 'There must have been someone looking after these creatures for a quite some time. Perhaps you are right with your suggestion of the king, the cook, and maid. The spell Brutus has put on these people and all the other infidels is a great help in the cause. Let's leave this horrible place. Just turn off all the electricity supply to the tanks and come back tomorrow.'

The two kittendogs agreed and all three left the laboratory, being only too glad to get some rest for the night.

*

At breakfast the next morning the trio was particularly quiet, and this was noticed by most of the others, especially Headeroonie Bill and Mickel, who eventually summoned enough courage to sit next to them. Anita took the lead and explained the revelations of the previous night. The result was one of utter disbelief, especially from Headeroonie Bill and Mickel, who both thought that everyone else should be told. An animated discussion then followed, the outcome of which came as a surprise to the original trio; only Jet was to be informed for the time being until further investigations were carried out. The problem was to break away from everyone else without creating suspicion, so a plan was devised to leave the table a few at a time at dishwashing time, and meet outside of the infidel canteen.

The plan duly worked and the group made their way to the laboratory discovered the night before. On reaching the door Anita produced the mystery key to gain entry. The Alisose wished to remain outside as a sentry, being too afraid at the prospect of visiting the laboratory once more.

The sight was not exactly pleasant to the unfortunate souls who had to cast their eyes over the carnage and desolation. The woodlice must have all died during the night, but not without an escape bid. Some had managed to crawl out of the tanks but had not got very far. Jet, not being used to the conditions, had trod on an expired woodlouse and the shell had split open, making a loud crunching noise. She bent over to pick up the pieces of shell, although this was made difficult by the slippery and slimy surroundings around the dead animal. Jet shined a torch over the evidence, and clearing away the mess, the inside of the shell could be seen. There was writing on the fragments, and the words "Training Academy" and "Department of Dirty Tricks" could be made out. This indicated that the shell was manufactured. The description was reminiscent of what had been found at the battle site where Mandy and Brutus had disappeared!

'What should we do now?' enquired Tonkas.

'I think we should tidy everything away so that it leaves the impression that nothing has been disturbed. I have taken the precaution of bringing preservative and syringes with me to inject into the dead woodlice. Then we should put them back into the same tanks they came out of, as much as possible. We could track the slime trails to help us do this. Next, switch the electricity back on and then clean the floor so no slime is left behind,' replied Anita.

All the kittendogs set about this task with mops and rags that Anita had also brought with her, using a bucket already in the laboratory. Tonkas filled the receptacle with water from a tap near a sink with was emptied and refilled several times until they were satisfied that a thorough job had been done.

Anita by this time had returned the woodlice back to their respective tanks, except for the smashed one which was placed in a polythene bag to be used for further investigation along with a sample of their food.

It was now time to take stock of the situation, and to gather the opinions of everyone present.

'I think we should have a good look around the place and perhaps take photographs as evidence,' said The Alisose.

'Good idea,' replied Tonkas. 'Let's see if there is anything else we can find.'

There appeared to be an office in the far corner of the laboratory, so it was decided to search this area first. The office was only large enough for one person to occupy at any one time. Inside there was a desk, chair, and computer together with a filing cabinet and bookshelf. Anita thumbed through some papers in a letter rack and discovered more evidence that the king was responsible for all that was going on in this laboratory. All the kittendogs had files on them arranged in alphabetical order of names, and there were location details of security cameras.

'This could be very useful information for us,' noted Anita. 'You had better take notes of where these cameras are and how to disable them.'

'We could copy the files from his computer, although it is probably password protected,' stated Tonkas.

'Perhaps we should do this another time in case infidels come back and we are caught in the act of stealing all this information. You can never be too certain of anything. We should leave as soon as we can and come back later. Now we need to keep a close eye on this area from now on. By entering this place last night we may have triggered a warning to the woodlice encampment. I repeat, it is better to be sure and leave as soon as possible now that the place is tidied,' said Anita.

Tonkas and The Alisose reluctantly agreed, though the two kittendogs stated that they had been lucky so far; all their activities having been undetected, even sleeping on the premises overnight.

'You cannot assume that you can get away with this for long,' said Anita. 'I think you should have a contingency plan in case anything goes amiss. Perhaps you could get in touch with Brutus to see if he can maintain his spell over the infidels, so we can carry on with your plans as well as building your own secret laboratory.'

The kittendogs felt happier with this and the entire group made their way out of the Manipulations Laboratory. In any case, lunch time was approaching, and it was thought that much was accomplished in the morning session.

Lunch time passed all too quickly and the latest news got around quickly. Although Jet was not best pleased that the secret was out, she was all too willing to help the kittendogs in their quest. Gregor also wished to volunteer as he joined Anita, Tonkas, and The Alisose deep in a conversation concerning the next plan of action.

Headeroonie Bill then arrived, insisting he should use the pigeoncats again on another reconnaissance mission, but this time trying to get closer to Brutus himself. Everyone consented with Headeroonie Bill, realising then any argument was futile. He always had his own way.

The group of five reconvened in the infidel laboratory to check over the pigeoncats and to recharge their batteries in readiness for another flight. Headeroonie Bill suggested that the mechanical birds should fly to the woodlice encampment, perch on a suitable tree, and relay information back. The most difficult and dangerous part was to establish a direct link with Mandy and Brutus and to ascertain how long the spell of Brutus could be maintained.

'I think the easiest thing to do is to write messages on paper and conceal them in a watertight and transparent case on the pigeoncat's legs. The next stage would be to attract the attention of Mandy and Brutus and somehow convey the message to them,' said Headeroonie.

'This is a very good idea,' agreed Anita. After a quick conversation, Headeroonie Bill and The Alisose were put in charge of the pigeoncats, Gregor writing the messages and fastening them to the legs. The others checked over the monitors and other electrical components necessary for this manoeuvre. After a while all appeared to be well.

'I would like to launch the pigeoncats again as I did before, and take The Alisose with me to check the sense of direction glands. The rest of you can stay behind and check over the monitors,' ordered Headeroonie Bill as he gathered the mechanical birds in his arms and strode out of the laboratory before anyone could answer.

Anita enquired whether this particular kittendog was always this bossy, to which the answer was in the affirmative.

'Never mind,' she said, 'better do what he says,' was the comment after he closed the door behind him. Gregor, Tonkas, and Anita could only look at the monitors and oversee the proceedings from the comfort of the laboratory. It was not very long before an image appeared on the screens of the lawn outside the building, of Headeroonie Bill launching the birds. The Alisose had performed her duties very well; jerky pictures became evident as the pigeoncats made their way to the encampment.

Unfortunately, the images stopped and the screens

went blank for a time, followed by grainy black and white lines accompanied by background crackling and hissing. Tonkas, Anita, and Gregor were becoming somewhat concerned and Tonkas was in a state of panic. They need not have worried however, as clear pictures gradually appeared after a short period of flashing on the monitors. This time the images were crystal sharp and truly amazing to the astonished and excited audience. There was both Mandy and Brutus in all their glory, appearing in excellent health. What was even more staggering was that in their paw-like hands were the messages written only a short time before. Brutus seemed to be in the act of replying by using the back of the paper, with what looked like a piece of charcoal.

'If only we could converse with them,' bleated Tonkas. 'When we get these pigeoncats back we must implant a microphone or something similar.'

'I could try and incorporate this into the sense of direction gland,' suggested The Alisose.

Just then, the pictures on the monitors flickered again and started to become grainy in appearance.

'It looks as though the lens can only focus at close range, otherwise the birds will have to fly back to a safer distance. Only Headeroonie Bill has the answer to all these questions, and I can only assume that they have been recalled by a blast of his whistle. The only action we can take is to wait for news,' said Anita.

The images faded from the monitors and the screens went black. The wait seemed interminable as, the ticking noise of the laboratory clock became louder and louder. No one said a word, nor did they want to; all the small group wished for was good news of Mandy and Brutus.

Their worries were to prove unfounded as Headeroonie Bill burst into the laboratory holding the pigeoncats and scraps of paper.

This action was greeted with a chorus of, 'Well done!' from the kittendogs, Anita, and also Gregor. The latter, in his haste to look at the writing on the paper, nearly tore it apart, snatching it away from Headeroonie Bill's grasp.

'Oh, do be careful. You could destroy the writing before we have a chance to look at it,' remonstrated Anita. She carefully unravelled the small pieces of paper and placed them on a flat surface. With one hand she smoothed the paper, being aware of possibly smudging the charcoal.

'It says, "We are doing fine despite being held in captivity," and yes, Brutus still has his powers of holding a spell. He is conscious of the situation but is holding the infidels under a time warp. They have no sense of time and every hour of their time is equivalent of ten of ours.'

'In that case their three-day conference will last for over a month and they will never know they have been away for all that time,' said Tonkas.

'This is really good news, we ought to inform everyone of what has happened, including the findings in the Manipulations Laboratory,' suggested The Alisose.

'Agreed,' replied Anita, who was gradually taking over the role of Headeroonie Bill at being in command of any decision making.

After another satisfactory morning's work lunch time was approaching once more and it was considered by everyone present that now was the time to have another session of recording and comparing all their findings.

At the infidel canteen Mickel was the only one present, who felt rather disappointed at the prospect at yet another meeting, little realising what was in store. When the revelations of the previous two days were revealed everyone was dumfounded. No one expected such a wicked laboratory existing in the building performing such heinous tasks. There was no shortage of volunteers for analysing the giant killer woodlice food, and replacing it with something that resembled it, but without the nourishing qualities. To that end a working party was set up with Miss Jet Drawls taking the lead. This was considered the only polite thing to do since she was the only representative of the Training Academy, apart from Anita, who remained loyal to the cause of the kittendogs. Gregor Nameless was to be second in command since he possessed a great deal of inside information that could be of great help. Mickel and Sylvate were to organise a watch on the Manipulations Laboratory along with Augustus and Serendipity. Everyone else was to help with the laboratory analysis of the woodlice food, although only a few hours of the afternoon and evening remained to make any progress on such an important task.

'What if intruders come into the Manipulations Laboratory?' asked Malter. 'They might realise that all the woodlice are dead. What about the food production? This should be substituted with a toxic substitute as soon as possible, otherwise the woodlice will continue to grow and multiply at the encampment.'

There followed a period of panic and mayhem at the possibility of an intrusion and so it was agreed that the working party on the food analysis would work around the clock, operating a shift pattern. It was at this point that the contents of the office were mentioned and that this could reveal more useful information. Anita elected herself group leader on this project with Tonkas and The Alisose helping as assistants. This group was abbreviated as Tat. Mareekoid was designated "chief of loose ends and nothing in particular", this activity being looked upon as commensurate with her attitude to life in general.

With all this being finally decided upon, the three groups set about their roles with an abundance of relish and enthusiasm.

The group on the surveillance of the Manipulations Laboratory called themselves Mass for short, this being the first letter of their names; Mickel, Augustus, Serendipity, and Sylvate.

'One does not seem to have much to do compared with the other groups unless invasions take place,' observed Augustus.

'It is still an essential activity,' noted Anita. 'I suggest two of you get some rest and the other two keep an eye on the den from a safe distance. Then change positions at some predetermined time which will be at your discretion. The Tat group can proceed with searching the king's office and perhaps some of the Mass group keep a lookout for them as part of the surveillance.'

After this comment the allotted groups went their separate ways, some of the kittendogs not best pleased with Anita's bossy attitude. Even Headeroonie Bill was rather put out, feeling his role was being usurped by a former infidel.

Best get on with what she wants, thought Tonkas, as he was followed by Anita into the laboratory.

'I would like to make a copy of the hard drive from the king's computer first of all,' said Anita. 'I have brought the necessary parts to do this, and I think it is better this way in case someone turns up unexpectedly. Leave everything as we found it. I can work on the contents in my own time at my leisure.' This left Tonkas and The Alisose to search through the papers to seek information.

'What are we looking for?' asked The Alisose.

'Look for anything to do with the giant killer woodlice,' answered Anita. 'This must be the priority, especially anything concerning the food. We need to determine what it is made of so we can alter it, to at least stunt their growth.'

'I think we need to weaken them so we could mount an attack on the encampment and rescue Mandy and Brutus. We can all then get back to normal,' suggested Tonkas.

'All in good time,' muttered Anita. 'Right, I have now got all the king's files on my memory devices so I can analyse the formula of the food. There are also files about you and other people, together with information about his surveillance cameras. This is really useful. Make copies of all the files you have found and then we can go and join the others.'

Tonkas did not like this idea as he considered it would take too long to complete the mission, so he protested. Luckily Anita saw the reasoning of his suggestion, and conceded that it would better to complete as much as possible.

'I see there are files appertaining to all the infidels, and even kittendogs, that you have selected. Just make sure that everything you have removed goes back in the exact order you found it. Now let's get back to our own lab.'

Mickel and Sylvate, who were guarding the premises from outside, gave an indication that the coast was clear and it was safe to leave the area. The working party, having completed their work successfully, left the area, removing paperwork.

'Phew, we managed to get our work completed without any mishap,' commented The Alisose. 'Let's get back to the others and tell them what progress we have made with the analysis of the woodlice food.'

'Right, I was going to say the same thing myself,' said Anita. 'I am hoping Jet and company have found what the ingredients are that make up the woodlice food, and what can be done to minimise or even prevent any of the effects it has.'

There was nothing more to be said on the issue, so the Tat group made their way to the infidel laboratory where the food analysis was taking place. They were greeted by Jet who was standing by the door assuming the role of sentry. 'Do come on in, goodness you have brought a lot of things with you,' as she stared at the trolley of items.

Once entry was gained Tonkas and The Alisose

were pointed in the direction of the office printer and scanner, and the pair set about the boring task of copying all the files that were temporary borrowed. In the meantime, Anita made her way to her own office, seeking some seclusion for the purpose of making some sense of the electronic files purloined from the king's domain. In essence this was the same as the paperwork that was in the possession of Tonkas and The Alisose: it was merely the format that was different.

Time was passing fast, and no one noticed it was lunch time, the food being prepared by Mareekoid who made herself productive in the kitchen. This was to everyone's utter surprise and delight since the morning's activities had resulted in a number of healthy appetites. It was also a good time for all the individual groups to catch up on each other and to compare and contrast their own conclusions.

To that end, Jet gave a short talk on the progress so far on food analysis using sophisticated laboratory instruments to determine the amounts of different constituents. The results of this were not quite ready, and rather than give misleading results it was felt better to present the findings later in the day. The other groups reached the same conclusion, so any further discussion was deemed unnecessary until further experimentation was completed.

On that bombshell, everyone simultaneously stood up as if controlled like puppets on strings and set about the boring task of clearing away dishes and the associated washing and drying. Tonkas was the only person to notice this strange event, thinking that perhaps Brutus was exercising his own special powers again, only this time working on friends rather than enemies.

There was one exception, however. Mareekoid exhibited her usual tendency to avoid any work, and seemed immune to the spell of Brutus. For the others the same robotic behaviour continued as the assemblage of personalities divided themselves into the previous groups, in order to continue the pre-lunch activities. Another thought passed through Tonkas's mind. Perhaps there was something in the cooking, even though it did not affect himself or his sibling.

The three groups set about their allotted tasks with renewed vigour, the food analysis group exhibiting a great deal of urgency as though the results were needed in extra quick time. Another thought occurred to Tonkas.

'Is there any chance of the woodlice food and our own food being mixed up?' he enquired. 'I was listening to your conversations and you are speaking somewhat differently and using longer words that usual.'

As a response to that comment, Mareekoid blushed profusely, as if admitting that a mistake had been made.

'I could have contaminated the utensils by not washing them properly,' she stuttered.

'Oh no,' groaned Tonkas. 'I must keep an eye on the food analysis group and check up on them to see if they are doing their work properly. The copying of paper files ought to stop for the time being, as well as Anita's computer hacking. I suggest that there is a minimal number of people guarding the

Manipulations Laboratory and everyone else join in on the food checking. The woodlice food is making most of us hyperactive.'

'This could be a clue in how to adapt the woodlice food,' suggested Anita. 'If we could remove this element perhaps we could slow them down so we could attack them,' she added, regaining some of her composure.

By now nearly everyone present was getting back to normal. Tonkas realised that the change caused by this food element was short-lived, when applied to beings other than woodlice. He thought it was still necessary to work on this particular element of the woodlice food. However, by now everyone knew the importance of this task and so there was feverish activity in order to achieve a satisfactory conclusion.

Finally, with all persons actively involved in the food analysis, a conclusion was reached, but not before every single instrument in the laboratory was used to its fullest extent. The chemicals in the woodlice food were identified, and one constituent seemed to be present in every single test. It was also discovered that this ingredient could be removed by fractional distillation more commonly used for oily substances, which indeed the woodlice food was. All the suitable laboratory glassware was used in the boiling and condensation of the obnoxious liquid, which was broken down into the constituent parts. In this way the element that caused the hyperactivity in the kittendogs was removed and kept separate from the rest of the compound. When the task was completed Anita and Jet called yet another meeting when the next course of action was to be debated.

Mareekoid was chosen as the unfortunate individual to try out the woodlice food without the separated ingredient, since she was responsible for the mixing of foods before lunch. With a great deal of chanting and coercion Mareekoid imbibed a glass of compound and everyone waited with bated breath to observe the outcome.

To the surprise of all those present Mareekoid suffered no ill-effects from partaking of this mysterious liquid that the woodlice seemed to thrive on.

Tonkas then appeared to have a brainstorm, bursting into an almost uncontrollable frenzy. 'Oh dear, oh dear, it's that word, Mana. It is Brutus again; we can expect unwanted visitors tonight in the Manipulations Laboratory!'

Anita was the first to reply. 'Quick, return the woodlice food to whence it came. Replace all the paperwork as well; I will gather all the copying that is finished. Make sure everything looks exactly the same as we found it, lock the door, and then wait.

CHAPTER 10

Invasion and Counter Invasion

Anita's orders were carried out very quickly, and everyone contributed to the best of their ability in the time available. The next decision was to allot tasks to the individuals present, and the mass group were to continue with surveillance on the Manipulations Laboratory. Augustus was the first to volunteer.

'One would like to have the first watch, although one would like Serendipity to accompany me because we are good friends, this would leave Mickel and Sylvate to take the second shift.'

Anita consented to this plan with the proviso that there should be a backup group, looking over the proceedings from the comfort of the security room. Anita wished to do this together with Tonkas and The Alisose from the raiders of the office group. This left the food analysis group to clear and tidy the laboratory, not forgetting the dreaded washing up. When this task was completed they were requested to retire for the night to get some rest in case reinforcements were required later in the night.

With the kittendogs and other persons located in their designated positions, those not required rested in their beds as best as they could. This proved to be difficult for many of them, since the excitement and apprehension levels were very high. Gradually, however, all settled down for the night, though the ticking of clocks seemed to become louder and louder. Those situated in the security room were starting to drift off to sleep, except for Anita, who was used to keeping long hours in her capacity of controller of infidels in the Training Academy laboratories.

It was Anita, with her super sensitive ears, who detected a slight noise from the corridor outside. Luckily everyone had already taken the precaution of sitting where they could not be spotted through the windows outside. The monitors were also facing away from outside so any images could not be seen.

'Why is it always me that notices any difference to the outside?' uttered Anita under her breath. She glanced at the monitors and noticed two smallish and strange-looking individuals carrying buckets and siphons with them, making for the Manipulations Laboratory.

'Goodness me, why were there no warnings from

Augustus and Serendipity? Good job I was awake.'

She nudged Tonkas and The Alisose gently, making sure they did not make a noise with an upright finger held close to her lips.

'We have company as you predicted, Tonkas, and they are heading to the laboratory where the woodlice food is being manufactured.'

Tonkas nodded, saying, 'I knew they would do this, otherwise why is that awful stuff being created in these premises? Somebody must move it from here to the encampment, so perhaps they cannot live without it. It is a good job we adulterated its composition last night, but we must watch what they do from now on.'

'What do you suggest?' was the reply from Anita and The Alisose simultaneously.

'This is rather difficult. For a start, why didn't Serendipity and Augustus give us a sign of the forced entrance? We need to find out what has happened to them, so one of us has to go to the outside of the Manipulations Laboratory to find out, while two of us stay behind or operate a relay system to inform each other.'

'I would like to go first,' volunteered Tonkas. 'I would like The Alisose to follow close behind in case anything should happen.'

Tonkas crept forward cautiously while The Alisose followed at a safe distance behind. Tonkas could make out two indistinct figures in the laboratory, which was illuminated by torches. He continued with his movements, making a diversion to another room opposite the laboratory where he knew Augustus and Serendipity were supposed to be on guard. Entering the room, huddled in the corner at the back were the two individuals, fast asleep. Quietly, he moved towards them and tapped on their shoulder at the same time. Both grunted and then awoke with a shudder.

'Oh, we are so sorry, we are so tired with all the work we have done and must have dozed off,' apologised Serendipity.

'Never mind, everything is alright. Now keep very quiet, there are unwanted guests around in the horrible place that has the dead woodlice. I don't want them to hear us,' sympathised Tonkas.

'One feels one has let the side down,' added Augustus.

Just then, The Alisose entered the room with the news that Anita had returned to the safety of the security room and gave instructions to remain still and let the invaders do what they wished.

'It is better to not interrupt them, otherwise it would arouse suspicion. Let them think that they have got away with it, since every movement is being recorded to identify them. Anita wants the invaders to return to the encampment with the falsified woodlice food and monitor want happens at their end using the pigeoncats.'

'Righto,' replied Tonkas. 'We will do this.'

The group waited patiently and quietly, not hearing or seeing anything for what seemed a very long time. Tonkas wanted to leave the room and investigate but the others forbade him.

'One must comply with Anita's orders and do what she wishes, resisting any temptation to disobey,' said Augustus.

As though the last comment was some sort of cue, there was a noise outside in the corridor of what seemed heavily laden feet and the sound of scraping.

'No one dare say anything or make any movement whatsoever until the coast is clear,' ordered Serendipity.

'How do we know when the coast is clear?'

'One thinks it is better to wait for a signal from Anita,' said Augustus.

'Very well,' was the reply from the others present.

Not for the first time that night did the wait seem long and tedious, some of the small group wishing to fall asleep with boredom. Eventually Anita turned up with the news that the invaders had departed and the next important task was to check the camera footage in the security room.

After carefully vacating the room which had been occupied for a long period of time, the group followed Anita to relative safety, not daring to look in the direction of the Manipulations Laboratory. Tonkas, The Alisose, Serendipity, and Augustus were all relieved to regain more comfortable surroundings, and refreshed themselves with drinks and food. The trauma had obviously had a detrimental effect on them.

After a period of relaxation all the characters resumed their previous duties, checking over the camera footage of the laboratory and corridor, even though they were all extremely tired.

At long last, the result everyone was wishing for was achieved – the two intruders were identified.

'Look at these images. These are two of the forest dwellers we thought were our friends. It is Umphadee and Umphadah!' exclaimed Tonkas.

'I really am very surprised at this; I used to play with them when I was much younger,' stated The Alisose. 'I thought I could trust them once but now they seem to be our enemies.'

'Perhaps we can track them down with the help of the pigeoncats, but this will have to be tomorrow. They have got a head start on us, it is dark outside and we are all very tired. We might as well call off the sentry duty on the Manipulations Laboratory and go to bed. Let's make a fresh start in the morning,' decided Anita.

*

The next morning began with a big announcement presented by Anita, with Jet in support, after breakfasting. Everyone attended the meeting, as it was deemed as the most important so far, since the start of the friendship between kittendogs and their sympathisers at the Training Academy. There was to be an inspection of the Manipulations Laboratory to determine what changes had happened the previous night. It was assumed that some or all of the woodlice food had been removed, otherwise what was the purpose of the buckets and siphons? Next, the whereabouts of the invaders needed to be determined. It was assumed that they must have made their way to the woodlice encampment to distribute the food and everyone wondered how long this had been going on. Finally, the most important question was, had the invaders noticed that the woodlice hatchlings were dead? To find the answer to at least some of these questions it was imperative to assess the changes to the Manipulations Laboratory.

Those present at the events of the previous night were elected to revisit the laboratory which was of so much interest to the invaders. Anita led the way as the others were still traumatised at the very thought of making an entrance without supervision and protection. The containers of woodlice food were diminished in contents, as was expected, but apart from that everything else appeared to be untouched.

'They must have just concentrated on the one task last night and forgot to check the infant woodlice,' noted The Alisose.

'They were in a hurry I expect,' suggested Tonkas. 'It is just as well they did not make any further investigation.'

'We need a plan to send the pigeoncats to the woodlice encampment, only this time to keep them there for some time to enable us to conduct a survey into their behaviour,' was a comment made by Anita.

'We need to see if the modified food has any effect on the woodlice and to see if they are weakened. If they become handicapped in any way we could attack them and hopefully rescue Mandy and Brutus,' added Tonkas.

Anita was, again, the next to speak. 'This is a rather hopeful idea. How do we know if the modified food has the desired effect? This would be a very lucky result.'

'One can only hope,' a voice said from the direction of the door. Of course it was Augustus who uttered these words, who added, 'All the others are wondering what you are getting up to all this time, and want you to impart your freshly gained knowledge.'

'In that case we should leave this dreadful place and return to the infidel canteen and continue with the announcements we began earlier,' agreed Anita.

Anita's suggestion was complied with and the group departed once more to inform the others of the latest findings, as Augustus wanted.

There followed a heated and protracted debate with everyone wanting to have their say in the matter. Headeroonie Bill was beginning to assert his authority over the kittendogs once more, since he thought he had a certain control over the pigeoncats and electric cuckoos. He also put his case forward that the pigeoncats should again be modified to enable an extension to the time they could spend in an unknown environment.

The Alisose volunteered without hesitation, realising she could gain more respect from her colleagues if she could improve upon her previous work that had so far performed well. Now was her chance to do even better and modify her design for the sense of direction glands, so that it could send more information, in a shorter space of time. There also remained the problem of more energy required to keep the mechanical birds at freedom for a longer period of time.

Anita then changed the subject by asking if the paperwork gleaned from the king's office was of any use to the cause. This action would leave Tonkas working on his own since The Alisose wanted to work on the birds.

At this point Anita opened, and said, 'I need additional help for Tonkas, it is not fair that he is on his own dealing with a mountain of paperwork.'

'I could put my special powers of observation to use,' was the reply. 'All I need is someone to place the paper in front of me and then remove it while I scan it with my eyes and brain. I need something like an automatic paper feeder, but it would be good to know what I am looking for.'

Anita answered, 'I know of such a thing in the office, I will go and fetch it. To give you some help I suggest you concentrate on the woodlice encampment, such as the exact location, and the lay of the land. We ought to mount a reconnaissance mission of our own and perhaps camp out overnight like you did before. If The Alisose modifies the pigeoncats again this would help as well.'

'Why don't we use the barnmobile like we did before and just use a small working party to spy?' said The Alisose.

'Good idea,' replied Anita, as Malter put his name forward to help Tonkas.

'I will get the automatic paper feeder if that's any help, if Anita shows me where it is,' said Mickel.

This was the order of the day from now on, as the two groups set about their tasks with much aplomb and vigour. They were much encouraged by recent events and were eager to find out the result of their endeavours concerning the modification of the woodlice food. There was a common aim between the two groups; that was to find out if the woodlice were weakened by eating the new food, provided it had been delivered by the invaders. There was only one way of finding out, this was to spy on the encampment and study their behaviour.

Tonkas, with his superb powers of rapid scanning, had uncovered the recipe for the woodlice food by the end of the day, and discovered that it could only be produced in laboratory conditions, thus confirming the reason for the invasion. This was a very good result since it exposed a serious weakness in the captors' defence. They could be starved into submission with any luck, reducing the need for an attack with possible casualties. Now that the next generation of these creatures had been exterminated hopefully the encampment was the only colony, and if they could be killed, any repetition of the battle could be averted.

The modifications to the pigeoncats were therefore an extra precaution, although it was useful to remain at a safe distance from the woodlice in case they were spotted. If the pigeoncats looked natural enough, the woodlice would not notice them. This in turn would assist in the reconnaissance mission and provide more information over a longer period of time.

The two teams worked independently of each other, Jet and Anita assuming overall control and offering leadership when it was required. This left the problem of the barnmobile since The Alisose had invented this contraption and knew how it worked. Headeroonie Bill was therefore placed in charge of getting the car ready for a return invasion as soon as possible. All these activities took the entire day and it came as a relief when it was time to stop, have something to eat, and then retire for the night for some rest and recuperation.

*

The next morning started as any other of recent days in the Training Academy, except that the atmosphere was full of anticipation and excitement. The problem lay in deciding who was going on the counter invasion, and who was staying behind. This was a contentious issue since there was not enough room in the barnmobile to seat everyone who wanted to go. The obvious choice was that the same personnel should be included as before because of the familiarity of the route. It was decided that Anita, Jet, and Gregor would remain behind since they were more of a part of the Training Academy, and could remain to oversee the operation from a safe distance. Tonkas and The Alisose were obvious choices for an invasion because the former had special powers and the latter was the only person who could drive the barnmobile. Headeroonie Bill was to lead the expedition as before, with Mareekoid in charge of the back-up group which included the ponies to carry luggage. The remaining kittendogs were Sylvate and Mickel, who wanted to go on the barnmobile as before, although Mareekoid could not be expected to attend to the ponies on her own. Augustus was elected to go along with the ponies and Mareekoid, since everyone was amused by his habit of using the word "one" very frequently.

With the personnel sorted out, the problem of provisions still remained, and the question was of how long to stay in the open air. Since this was only to be another reconnaissance mission, although somewhat longer this time, extra time would be required to monitor the effects of the woodlice food.

The preparations were thus completed under the guidance of Jet, Anita, and Gregor, and at least this time there was not the spying eyes of the cook and maid to contend with or time constraints.

The Alisose spent little time extricating the barnmobile from its garaging quarters, and preparing it for its trip. It needed some attention as it had not been used for a few days. She also spent considerable time reacquainting herself with the controls and making sure the wings were ready in case they were needed.

All was well; the barnmobile was ready for its latest adventure and was duly packed with the entire essentials for at least two nights in the open air. After the baggage, the last to be loaded were the kittendogs, with The Alisose in the driving seat and Tonkas alongside. This left Headeroonie Bill, Mickel, and Sylvate in the rear, together with what luggage could be accommodated, with any leftover items given to Mareekoid and Augustus to be loaded on the ponies.

Jet, Anita, and Gregor insisted on giving everything a final check even though they were not present at the first expedition. The main reason for their presence was to see them off, wishing them every success even though the mission was hopefully for a short period of time. The Training Academy friends had established a good rapport with the kittendogs over the last few days, and Anita was reluctant to signal farewell. However, the quest had to continue, and sentiment had to be cast aside for the sake of the safe return of Mandy and Brutus.

With a lump in her throat Anita gave them a final wave as the entourage moved slowly off, in order that Mareekoid, Augustus, and the ponies could keep up with the potentially faster moving barnmobile. As they disappeared from sight Anita finally realised the depth of her attachment to this strange group of individuals, and the entertainment and character they had shown. With a final sigh she turned on her heels in the direction of the Training Academy, and with a heavy tread made her way back to the laboratory with Jet and Gregor close behind. The best she could do for them now was to act as a distant guide, constantly looking after them with the modern technology prevalent in the comfort of the security room.

'All we can do now is to wait and see what happens. I am so glad they have the pigeoncats with them to give them extra support. I hope they have the sense not to get too close to the giant killer woodlice encampment,' Anita informed her two compatriots, not realising that the kittendogs had done exactly that in their previous close encounter with the enemy. It was decided to operate a shift pattern in the security room so that nothing was missed. Anita offered to take the first shift while Jet and Gregor made their way to the infidel canteen for refreshments.

In the meantime, the barnmobile, ponies, and the occupants were making steady progress towards the objective, which was the same campsite they used before. The greatest difficulty was the battle site, which was full of bad memories for the kittendogs, the worst being the disappearance of Mandy and Brutus. This was passed at a greater speed than the rest of the journey to make the mental pain easier to bear. In a short time, the original overnight stop was reached, the barnmobile this time not employing its wings but remaining on solid ground so that the ponies could remain a short distance behind.

The group made the wise choice to remain in familiar surroundings, and the contents of both the barnmobile and ponies were unpacked to prepare sleeping quarters for the night. Headeroonie Bill wished to remain in charge of the pigeoncats. The Alisose was insistent on checking the sense of direction glands, setting them to the same coordinates as before, assuming that the woodlice had not moved the encampment to a different location. After some more final checks, Headeroonie Bill and The Alisose agreed to release the mechanical birds on their way, remaining in radio contact at all times using a monitor they had brought from the Training Academy. At first the images obtained were grainy and indistinct, but the quality improved and after a final flicker the encampment was plainly seen. Every other activity stopped with immediate effect, as all the kittendogs gathered around the monitor as best they could, when the terrible woodlice appeared on the screen. To everyone's great pleasure the movement of the woodlice seemed very sluggish, compared to what was observed on the previous occasion.

A sigh of relief went around the group. It was obvious that the change of diet was having its effect.

'I think now is the best time to recall the pigeoncats, let them rest overnight to recharge their batteries, and also to relay images back to Anita to let her know how we are getting along,' suggested Headeroonie Bill with a hint of his former bossiness.

The rest agreed as this was a reasonable idea, and it was better to set up camp when it was still daylight just as they did before when the plan worked successfully.

'How about setting up some sort of guard in case the woodlice detect anything and attack us?' enquired Tonkas.

'I have already thought of that. The pigeoncats have been programmed to leave a camera in one of the trees overlooking their camp. This will relay images to a monitor fitted inside the barnmobile, and again we will have to arrange an all-night vigil to make sure nothing untoward happens. A shift pattern is called for yet again, operating in pairs, until tomorrow morning when we will reassess the situation,' responded Headeroonie Bill, getting even bossier with every sentence.

'Ok, good idea, let's get on with setting up our camp first before recalling the pigeoncats,' replied Tonkas.

After the usual mumbling amongst the kittendogs the plan was carried out, with a number of tents being erected in a row, and the barnmobile concealed with a covering of plastic sheeting. This was then sprayed with camouflage paint, allowing a gap for entrance. The same procedure was then repeated for the tents until nearly everything was concealed to make it virtually invisible to anyone passing by. The location was rather remote so it was unlikely anything would be spotted, but it was thought better to err on the side of caution. When this was done, Headeroonie Bill summoned the pigeoncats with his whistle in the usual manner and they duly arrived in a short time. The first thing to do was to switch them off and charge their batteries overnight using the charger in the barnmobile. Sylvate and Mickel offered to take the first shift and the others settled down for the night.

The hours of darkness passed peacefully and without incident, punctuated only by the changeover of kittendogs involved in sentry duty. Apart from that there was only noise from animals foraging in the woods, and the rustling of leaves in the gentle breeze. For some members of the group the anticipation was too great, for they found it difficult to rest, wondering what lay in store in the following day. Just as the unfortunate individuals concerned were drifting off to sleep, it was time to get up again as daylight approached. One other factor was the constant snoring of Sylvate, which only affected Mickel and no one else.

It was Mickel who was the first to get up, finally succumbing to the snoring and wanting to escape from the originator. He wandered off to where the pigeoncats had last been stored following the shutting down procedure, and noticed that they had gone.

A voice said behind him, 'If you are looking for those birds I have sent them off on another mission to see if there are any new developments. I have reprogrammed them to assimilate data in the way of images in storage containers clamped to their feet. You can see I have been busy in the night while you have been asleep. Now wake up the others while I get some well-deserved rest. You lot can get dressed and prepare breakfast ready for the pigeoncats' return. Don't bother me until this event occurs.'

'Yes boss, right away, sir,' recognising the voice as

Headeroonie Bill's. 'I will do this straight away,' was the answer from Mickel, who thought he had better flatter him lest he be offended by anything other than subservience.

Mickel did as he was bid and awoke everyone else in the camp, Mareekoid actually doing something useful by cooking full English breakfasts for those interested in consuming this sort of food early in the morning. The ravenous kittendogs consumed the offerings with much relish; the fresh air had given them a good appetite. Unbeknown to the group Headeroonie Bill had satisfied himself in that department much earlier, having found the time to both eat and modify the pigeoncats while everyone else was senseless to the goings on.

Eventually breakfasting was completed, and also the associated washing of the dishes and the clearing away. Tonkas, as if by magic, awoke just as the last of the necessary work was finished and was ready to give his orders once again.

'It is time to release the pigeoncats now that their batteries are fully charged, and the reprogramming is satisfactory. Come and witness the quality of my workmanship when the birds are sent on a new fact-finding mission that could very well result in the freedom of your parents.'

'Good grief, he is becoming more arrogant than ever, and so confident that his work is good enough to bring all this about. I do not share his feelings, but we must at least try,' mumbled Tonkas to himself.

The other kittendogs, although disinclined to share the thoughts of Tonkas, nevertheless followed

Headeroonie Bill and the pigeoncats to a suitable site where the birds were again set free on this new mission.

'Have patience with our self-appointed leader,' whispered The Alisose. 'He has done so much for us in our quest to find Mandy and Brutus and perhaps we have reached a turning point. We must find out if the altered food will have its desired effect on those dreadful woodlice creatures that have been changed by the king beyond all recognition.'

'I agree with the last statement,' answered Tonkas. 'Those woodlice were so small and helpful in the compost pits in the gardens of the mansion house. I cannot understand why this person would do this against the innocents.'

'What is all this mumbling about, you two? We must wait now for a while for the pigeoncats to do what I have asked of them. In the meantime, let us tidy the camp; we may have to leave in a hurry,' stated Headeroonie Bill.

To placate him, everyone obeyed the latest orders and the camp was tidied of all the cooking utensils and leftover food. This was followed by the packing away of the tents, although some of the kittendogs thought this was a little hasty in case the items were needed for another night in the open air. Headeroonie Bill was aware of the uncomfortable atmosphere and added that he thought Anita was very concerned for their welfare, and the sooner they were all back safe and sound, the better it would be.

The next activity was to remove the camouflage from the barnmobile and the pony enclosure so hastily erected the night before.

As the last of the plastic sheets were being folded away, the pigeoncats flew into the camp right on cue, as though Headeroonie Bill knew this was going to happen. The birds were greeted with whoops of delight as it was observed that small canisters were attached to their legs, and their beaks full of more artefacts which were quickly deposited on the front seat of the barnmobile.

Headeroonie Bill wasted no time in retrieving the objects, selecting one at random and plugging it into the screen at the front of the vehicle. As soon as he did this, images on the monitors became evident of the giant woodlice staggering about in a disorganised manner. Headeroonie Bill then extracted a small piece of paper from one of the canisters on the bird's leg. It was a note written by Brutus with the information that both he and Mandy were both safe, and to hurry back with smudge bombs to finish the job. He added that if this was done the return of Mandy and Brutus was assured.

'Quickly,' Headeroonie Bill stated. 'We have no time to lose. Go back to the Training Academy and mansion house and collect all the smudge bombs and people you can find. The end of the mission is in sight.'

CHAPTER 11

The Rescue

The group of kittendogs were ecstatic when they heard of the exciting news and looked forward to a satisfactory conclusion to all their hard work. Everything had been prepared for a speedy departure; Headeroonie Bill must have had prior knowledge that this was going to happen.

The final checks were undertaken on the barnmobile to enable a rapid return to the mansion house where the smudge bombs were stored. It was agreed that the ponies could stay behind for the time being as they would only slow down the barnmobile, which was to return with its original crew, leaving Mareekoid and Augustus behind.

The Alisose got into the driver's seat of the vehicle, beckoning to the others to hurry and also get in. The plan was to return to the mansion first to collect the unused smudge bombs, and secondly go to the Training Academy to inform Anita, Jet, and Gregor.

With the minimum of fuss, the small band of kittendogs set off once more, although this time it was rather different. There was little chance of being pursued by the enemy and it was felt time was on their side despite Headeroonie Bill's comments. By now the route had become very familiar so this made things easier, and there was no need for The Alisose to use her sense of direction gland. This time it was not necessary to utilise the wings of the vehicle; the rough track was easier to use following a spell of dry weather. Following a brief conversation on the way, Sylvate, Mickel, and Tonkas were to get off at the mansion house to gather the armaments. In the meantime, The Alisose was to contact Anita and inform her of the good news.

The plan was soon to be initiated as the mansion house was reached, and a short stop was made for Tonkas and the others to get off and initiate a search for smudge bombs. The Alisose carried on to the Training Academy premises, and the barnmobile was parked at the rear of the building. A search was then made for Anita, The Alisose rushing up the stairs to the laboratories where their friends worked. As if by chance, Anita was locking the main doors of the laboratory complex and was very pleased to see at least one of the kittendogs.

'Where are the rest of you?

The Alisose explained the latest situation, giving all

the details and requesting her help in an assault on the woodlice encampment.

'Of course, and I will enlist Jet and Gregor. But first l will need the van to use both as a conveyance for any weaponry and the personnel. You will find the gang in the infidel canteen. Go and fetch them and l will see you back here in ten minutes while l fetch the van.'

The pair left at the same time, going in separate directions to fulfil their respective tasks. After the allotted time elapsed, Anita arrived first, a little red in the cheeks caused by the effort she had made. She waited for a while rooted to the spot, but her impatience got the better of her. Anita made her way back to her laboratory and the adjoining office. To her surprise the individuals were there instead of the meeting place that had been arranged earlier.

'Oh, how nice to see you,' was the somewhat sarcastic comment on the reunion, to which the recipients were somewhat surprised. Anita was always pleasant, at least up to the present time.

'I have the Training Academy van ready for our instant departure, and l hear you wish to stop off at the mansion to collect some sort of weapons to attack the woodlice. I have taken the precaution of adding some catapults to launch these bombs of yours, but I have to say I am frightened to be involved in any sort of battle. I only hope you are sure that it is safe to attack these creatures.'

This would appear to account for Anita's behaviour, thought The Alisose, and then she continued aloud, 'Never mind, you need not be involved in any fighting, just help us out with the munitions.'

'Alright, perhaps l can cope with that,' Anita replied as she got into the driver's seat of the van and drove off after The Alisose got into the passenger seat.

The journey to the mansion was uninteresting, but nevertheless essential for the greater scheme of things. As soon as the destination was reached the pair alighted from the van and lost no time in starting a search for the other kittendogs.

However, there was no need as Sylvate and Mickel appeared from nowhere with both their arms waving frantically to attract attention.

'Quick, come with us, Tonkas has found all the unused smudge bombs but needs help to get them downstairs,' they wailed uncontrollably, afraid that the bombs could explode at any time.

The Alisose and Anita were the first to get out of the van and then they rushed to the back door of the mansion and upstairs to Tonkas's bedroom. There was assembled a plethora of different size smudge bombs all lying on the floor.

'Help me get these downstairs, l have just found them lying around on the roof. They must have been left behind after the battle and there are enough of them to finish the job. There are too many of them to handle on my own, but if we can get the bombs to the encampment we can defeat the giant killer woodlice with any luck.'

The Alisose and Anita readily agreed, recognising the importance of this statement. They eagerly gathered as many bombs as they could, having long before being made safe after the great battle. Only a simple operation was required to make them operative once more. The trio made their way carefully down the stairs to the back door and into the open air and relative safety. After checking once more that the bombs were safe to handle, the collection was deposited into the back of the van. This was repeated a number of times until all the bombs were transferred from the mansion into the van, each one being checked for safety reasons, Anita being very frightened at the thought of driving the van with such a potentially dangerous load.

Her thoughts had to be put to one side, however, to concentrate on the task of driving to the encampment, following the barnmobile all the way. The route proved more difficult for the van than the barnmobile because of the uneven nature of the track. It was lucky that the bombs were carefully packed and they did not move about very much.

'Stop at our campsite where Headeroonie Bill, Mareekoid, and the ponies are waiting for our return. We should then decide on what to do next, depending what has happened since we have been away. Perhaps the pigeoncats can be sent on another mission to find out what the giant woodlice have been doing,' said The Alisose.

Anita merely nodded her head to signify that she understood, placing all her attention on her driving. She was quite determined to get to the destination safely, heedful of the dangerous cargo. Not wishing to jeopardise the plan, Anita did not divert her head from the road ahead, and nothing was going to break her concentration. The Alisose decided to say nothing else, and the atmosphere inside the van became fraught and very tense until at last the barnmobile appeared in sight, with its occupants just getting out of the vehicle.

'Ah, there you both are, I hope you have brought something useful with you,' questioned Headeroonie Bill as he approached the van, with the driver's window already wound down and Anita's face protruding from it.

'But of course,' was the reply. 'I wouldn't dream of coming here without bearing gifts. Is there any news regarding the status of the giant woodlice?'

'I can confirm that the creatures you mentioned are in a state of decline to say the least, though we should approach them with a great deal of caution. When you were away I took the liberty of making some spears from tree branches, and also amassed some large rocks, small enough for us to handle but heavy enough to crush the woodlice shells. I sent the pigeoncats away but they soon came back confirming the news that I have just conveyed to you. All we need to do is to repack the smudge bombs onto the ponies, carry as much as we can, and walk the rest of the way to the outskirts of their village.'

'Righto,' was the answer from Anita, in an unconvincing tone of voice. 'Let's get together what we need for the assault and to this effect I will unload the van.'

Getting out of the vehicle, Anita sauntered to the rear and The Alisose did the same on her side. The two of them met at the rear, Anita carefully opening the doors. The bombs lay as they were packed, surviving the journey unscathed. The ponies were summoned by Mareekoid who was standing just a short distance away in the campsite area, and the bombs were loaded into saddle bags which had previously been emptied of their contents.

This left the other kittendogs, Tonkas, Sylvate, and Mickel, to carry whatever they could in the way of weaponry leaving Headeroonie Bill in the lead position which suited him admirably. He insisted on taking a pigeoncat on each shoulder, leaving his hands free to hold some spears doubling up as walking sticks. The group was therefore prepared for the walk to the encampment, following their leader in a single line fashion, along a narrow path bordered on both sides by small trees and shrubs. The latter excluded most of the natural light and so made the walk rather gloomy and creepy. The silence was only broken by footsteps on the hard ground and the birdsong in the distance stimulating the pigeoncats into activity. Without any control from the owner the birds adjusted their wings and then took off, resisting any attempt by Headeroonie Bill to stop them.

'Oh no, these birds are developing minds of their own, I did not ask them to leave without my permission,' moaned Headeroonie Bill.

'Perhaps that wasn't birdsong after all. It could have been Mandy or Brutus mimicking, and perhaps we should hurry up and get to the woodlice encampment,' suggested Tonkas.

Without any further ado this idea was put into good effect; the pace increased, and a greater sense of urgency prevailed. Headeroonie Bill, by this time was becoming increasingly worried that the pigeoncats were gone for good, such was his concern. The pace quickened even more and the leaders had separated from the main group, with Anita in the rear. Soon they became somewhat surprised when the pigeoncats flew past, performed a circular sweep and then landed on Headeroonie Bill's shoulders in the same position that they had occupied before. This time they brought something back with them in the form of scribbled notes attached to their feet. Headeroonie Bill stopped in his tracks in an instant, his mouth wide open in surprise. In fact, he stopped so suddenly that Tonkas, following in hot pursuit, nearly collided with him.

The pieces of paper were quickly opened by the recipient and read with even more haste. Headeroonie Bill gave a big hurray and frantically waved the paper in the air.

'Look, it is exceedingly good news! Both Mandy and Brutus are safe and well although they are locked in a shed. The birdlike noise we heard was indeed them communicating with us, or rather the pigeoncats, who got in the shed through an open window. The notes also state to mount an attack straight away since the woodlice have become very weak with hunger, and are in no condition to fight. Victory is in sight!'

This comment provided the impetus for the group to quicken their pace even more, and Anita seemed to regain her courage. With feelings running high, the end of the narrow path came into view. Beyond this lay an open field with a dry wall around its perimeter. In the far distance were igloo structures, with a road on the horizon.

'I think we should split up and hide behind the wall, and then decide what to do from there. If we are too far apart wait for a signal from me in the guise of a raised spear,' said Headeroonie Bill.

'Ok,' was the reply from the kittendogs nodding in agreement as they crept slowly forward until the shelter of the wall was reached.

From that position a very short set of instructions were given by Headeroonie Bill, and three separate groups occupied different sections of the wall. After a short while, Headeroonie Bill raised a spear and the three groups leapt over the wall to initiate an attack. Anita was still frightened and elected to stay behind to act as a rear guard.

'Wait a minute, in our haste we have forgotten about the smudge bombs. We need to distribute them evenly amongst the groups and also the catapults which Anita brought,' said Headeroonie Bill.

'You also forgot about me and the ponies,' said a voice. 'I have just caught up with you and I have the bombs you just mentioned. Anita has just supplied me with the catapults.'

Mareekoid sounded annoyed and a little distressed with the thought that the group had marched on with gathering speed, forgetting about her and the dangerous cargo the ponies carried.

By now the kittendogs had jumped back over the wall and sat down behind it to conceal themselves from the encampment.

'You will jeopardise the mission if you keep talking like this, the enemy could hear us. Unload the bombs and catapults and divide them between the groups. Tie the ponies up where they cannot be seen and then start again,' said Headeroonie Bill.

Tonkas was the first to act as he grabbed the reins of the ponies from Mareekoid and ushered them to the edge of the field from whence they came.

'Hurry up, we are losing precious time with this delay, we need to get on with things.'

Tonkas tied up the ponies and then rushed towards the others, thrusting the smudge bombs and catapults into the open hands of the others, urging them to organise themselves into three groups.

'We need to attack very soon from as many different directions as we can, all at the same time,' he continued as he pushed the stationary kittendogs in the direction of the wall. Grabbing hold of their arms one at a time, he divided them into three groups of two individuals, leaving Anita out of the proceedings as he declared her unsafe to attack.

At that point Headeroonie Bill wanted a piece of the action and dearly wanted to assume control one more time, raising a spear in a vertical position to initiate the attack.

'Wait!' screamed Tonkas, and again he pushed his siblings into pairs and pointed them in the vicinity of where he desired the assault to take place.

'Right, let's go,' and leading the first charge with catapult and smudge bomb at the ready, Tonkas made for the centre of the encampment with Headeroonie Bill veering off to his left with Mickel in tow. Mareekoid and Sylvate had by now overcome their natural tendency of inertia and made to the right, where there were a lesser number of igloo structures. The Alisose rushed towards Tonkas and the strategy was complete. The first to reach the enemy was

Headeroonie Bill, his long legs propelling him faster than anyone else. Observing a giant woodlouse staggering about uncontrollably, he thrust his raised spear at the shell, piercing it easily. The creature gave out a long and high-pitched scream, raised itself on its legs, and then with a final sigh rolled over upside down and breathed its last. Tonkas, observing this success, did the same when another of these terrible creatures appeared.

All this had a knock-on effect as the other kittendogs sensed that the giant woodlice had become vulnerable. They repeated the same action, slaughtering everything that resembled the enemy that happened to stumble in their path. The supplies of spears were quickly exhausted, leaving only the smudge bombs left. Catapults at the ready, Headeroonie Bill and each of the kittendogs mounted a coordinated assault on the woodlice, each and every bomb finding its target with great precision. The weapons had an immediate effect by neutralising the woodlice, and stopping them in their tracks. Although not totally exterminated, the woodlice would play no further role in the battle and would be finished off at a later stage.

By now there were very few of the woodlice left, even being outnumbered by the attacking force. The end of the enemy was now in sight as the remaining pests were cornered at the wall, where they were to be beaten by small rocks as the smudge bombs became fewer in number. The final woodlouse was dispatched by a recycled spear and that was the end of the matter.

'What do we do now?' asked Tonkas.

Before he could answer, Mickel grabbed a small

rock and smashed it against the nearest dead woodlouse, breaking its shell very easily. From the woodlouse oozed a gelatinous fluid which smelt like rotten eggs, which Mickel ignored, such was the intent and vigour of destroying utterly the horrible creature. With his paw-like hands he tipped the shell over to enable the remainder of the contents to drain away, and peered at the interior.

'I thought so. The shell has been stamped by the king indicating that it was the property of the Department of Dirty Tricks, and I expect all the others have been treated in the same way. We must find out.'

The other kittendogs, with Headeroonie Bill leading, gathered the slain woodlice into a centralised area and used anything they could lay their hands on to crack open the shells just as Mickel had done. Each one had the same stamp on its interior, giving the impression that the woodlice were somewhat artificial. Such was the disrespect shown towards these beastly things that the remains were piled into a heap in the centre of the battle area.

'Let's set fire to them,' suggested Mickel.

'Aren't you forgetting something, such as the reason we came here in the first place?' said The Alisose.

'Of course, we have completely forgotten about Mandy and Brutus. We must find them as soon as possible. Look for a building that looks like a barn or shed,' answered Tonkas.

'You have also forgotten about the igloos,' said a female voice. It was Anita, who had finally summoned the courage to make an appearance now that the fighting was over.

'There may be woodlice still inside,' she added.

Headeroonie Bill volunteered to enter the first igloo on his own, taking the initiative and making Anita feel very ineffective at the same time. What he found surprised him in that the structure was deserted, although there was a foul-looking liquid on the floor which resembled that found in the Manipulations Laboratory.

'The creatures must have been badly affected by the altered food stolen by Umphadee and Umphadah,' he stated.

'We need to indicate which igloo, so that is not reoccupied,' suggested The Alisose.

'Let's demolish each igloo we inspect so the woodlice cannot use it again,' answered Tonkas.

This proved to be quite easy as the spears were employed once more, each kittendog piercing the thin shell of the igloo with continuous stabbing, working in a clockwise direction and moving around in a circle until the whole structure collapsed on itself in a cloud of dust.

'We need to do this to every igloo and this will take some time,' observed Headeroonie Bill. 'In the meantime we must find Mandy and Brutus.'

'Why don't I stand guard over the igloos while the rest of you look for Mandy and Brutus?' suggested Tonkas.

'I will help, you can't be a sentry on your own,' added The Alisose.

'Very well then,' decided Headeroonie Bill. 'I hope

nothing happens, and don't go inside any of them.

The remaining kittendogs gathered around Headeroonie Bill and made for the back of the camp away from the igloos since they all looked the same. From previous information it looked as though Mandy and Brutus were imprisoned in another type of structure and there was nothing to be gained in that respect of looking around igloos.

As the group approached the rear of the camp, the ground dropped away steeply, masking what appeared to be a shed with a tall watchtower alongside it. Around the two structures were dead or dying woodlice, obviously affected by the food they had been given since there were slime trails everywhere.

'I wonder if Umphadee and Umphadah knew that this food would affect the woodlice in this way; it could explain why the mystery key was on Anita's key ring. After all, it was discovering the Manipulations Laboratory that resulted in us altering the food. In turn that has led to their demise,' postulated Headeroonie Bill.

'It could explain why Anita's behaviour has changed recently when we suggested attacking this camp. I think she knows more than she lets on,' said Mickel.

Before anything else could be added a series of screams came from the direction of the buildings. This was accompanied by, 'Mana, Mana,' over and over again.

'It must be Brutus crying for help,' said Mickel, and he reached the shed and gave the door a heavy kick with an upraised foot. He lost his balance, and fell over something lying on the floor. It was Mandy and Brutus lying on the floor!

Brutus gave a grunt and mumbled, 'Mana,' several times over in a quiet, almost indiscernible voice before waking. By now Mickel had got up from the floor, though was still resting on his knees with one hand on Brutus's shoulder and one on Mandy's. Giving both of them a shake, his parents finally came to their senses and gave Mickel a big hug. Brutus managed to speak a little.

'Oh Mickel, we have missed you so much. We were both captured in a great battle with ugly creatures, and were carried away against our will. We left clues on how to find us and I guess you found them otherwise you would not be here. We are very tired and may lose our special powers if we are not revived soon. Oh, for some fresh water at least.'

With that, Brutus passed out again, and Mickel made an exit from the shed.

In the meantime, the rest of the kittendogs had congregated outside the shed, fearful of making an entry in case something untoward was going to happen to them. Headeroonie Bill was again the first to make any sort of comment, although his face was so contorted with dread that he only mumbled a few words. No one heard anything of use to them.

'Pull yourself together you lot, am I the only person doing anything useful around here?' bellowed Mickel. Continuing with his angry tone of voice, he ordered Headeroonie Bill and anyone standing close by to fetch some water. 'It could be a matter of life or death.'

Anita then appeared from the back of the

gathering holding two containers of liquid.

'I heard what you said and brought some supplies with me. These containers are so heavy and have been slowing me down. That is why I have been so long getting here.'

'We thought you were too scared to be involved in the fighting,' said Mickel.

'Perhaps I was,' was the reply.

'Enough of all this, we need to get the water to Mandy and Brutus as soon as possible.' Mickel grabbed the two containers and re-entered the shed. Raising their heads in turn, he held one of the containers to both Mandy and Brutus and slowly managed to energise the couple. They slowly became strong enough to stand on their feet. The final act was to release them from their bonds, and both Mandy and Brutus staggered outside to receive a tumultuous welcome.

Although weak through lack of food, Mandy and Brutus acknowledged the cheering, managed a feeble wave, and sensing a possible misadventure, Anita rushed over to steady them. Thus she exhibited the compassionate side of her nature and ushered them towards a safer area in the form of a flat rock on which they could rest awhile.

'I think I should fetch the barnmobile and fly them back to either the mansion or the Training Academy for some medical aid,' suggested The Alisose.

Anita replied, 'The Training Academy would be better, Jet would only be too willing to help, but you need to take someone else with you as support.'

Mareekoid then added to the discussion by suggesting the ponies could be used to get back to the barnmobile in order to quicken things along. 'Then I could return with the ponies while The Alisose drives the barnmobile back.'

'Brilliant idea,' added Anita. 'I will keep a close eye on Mandy and Brutus while the rest of you inspect the rest of the igloos to make sure there are no giant woodlice around.'

Headeroonie Bill and Mickel immediately turned on their heels and made for the nearest igloo. This left Sylvate and Tonkas the only unoccupied kittendogs, so they also volunteered to do the same and made for the second igloo.

Eventually all the igloos were checked over in this manner, the few woodlice that were found were already dead, and were dragged out into the open air to join the carcasses of the creatures already slain in the battle. Each igloo thus inspected in this manner was demolished by any means possible. The activity left the four kittendogs involved exhausted, though they were thoroughly satisfied with their work.

Mickel then had a brainwave. 'Why don't we set the woodlice carcasses on fire? In that way the smoke can act as a beacon for The Alisose to find her way back. You never know, her sense of direction gland could malfunction.'

'Another brilliant idea, let's do this,' was the comment made by Headeroonie Bill.

The task was set about with much enthusiasm; there was plenty of combustible material lying around in the form of sticks and fallen leaves. This formed the base of the intended fire with a few of the deceased woodlice placed carefully on top. The next stage was to find a source of ignition. It was suggested that the rubbing of sticks could produce the all-important spark. However, Headeroonie Bill had a better idea. He had noticed a broken bottle lying nearby and holding it in a suitable position, he managed to burn a hole in a leaf using the sun's rays. It was indeed fortunate that it was a sunny day, otherwise their luck would have run out at this point.

The effect was quite staggering, catching everyone by surprise. A pile of leaves very rapidly caught alight, setting some twigs on fire, followed by the first of the dead woodlice. Flames and smoke shot up into the air, and more woodlice were added, making the fire even bigger.

'Careful this doesn't attract unwanted attention,' said Headeroonie Bill. Just as he uttered these words Mareekoid appeared with the two ponies and gasping, she said, 'The Alisose got Mandy and Brutus into the barnmobile and took off for the Training Academy. Let's hope she is back soon, and we can all go home and leave this awful place.'

'I quite agree,' replied Mickel. 'I would like to do one more thing before we go and that is to utterly destroy the woodlice creatures and to eradicate anything to do with the Department of Dirty Tricks nonsense.'

'Well, alright, but we are drawing attention to ourselves, so let the flames die down a bit and in the meantime gather together all the woodlice and igloo bits in a heap near the fire. Place the pieces on the flames gradually,' replied Headeroonie Bill.

All the fit and able kittendogs diverted their energy to the latest request and the job was completed just as darkness was setting in.

'What should we do if any woodlice have escaped? They might start breeding, and then we would have to start this sorry business all over again,' said Mickel.

'There is no time to worry about that. Look, I can see the barnmobile above us. Clear the area and make room and then place all the rubbish on the fire,' ordered Headeroonie Bill.

Again the kittendogs did as they were bid, making the fire burst into flames once more.

'I think it is time to go. Pile into the barnmobile and let's go to the Training Academy. We all need to find out how Mandy and Brutus are doing,' added Headeroonie Bill.

CHAPTER 12

The Aftermath

By now curiosity had got the better of the occupants of the barnmobile regarding the fate of Mandy and Brutus. The Alisose drove to the Training Academy and parked to the rear of the buildings, next to the van that Anita had driven there a short time before. Tonkas was the first to get out of the vehicle, and rushed up the stairs to the laboratory complex where he knew Anita and Jet would be treating Mandy and Brutus. However, before he could enter any of the rooms he encountered Anita in the corridor. Before he could say anything himself, she was the first to speak.

'Your parents are doing just fine, but need plenty

of rest. Bear in mind Brutus should not be disturbed for now otherwise his special powers will be compromised, and the infidels might find their way back. There is still much to be done. He and I both agree that the papers from the king's office should be inspected more thoroughly. He also suggests that anything to do with the woodlice should be destroyed. However, it is getting late now, and much progress has been made today. Now it is time for you all to rest and continue with the work tomorrow. Hopefully Mandy and Brutus will be fully recovered by then.'

The rest of the kittendogs were just coming up the stairs and most of the leaders in the chasing pack had heard what Anita had just related to Tonkas.

'It is better we all rest for the night,' Headeroonie Bill said to the rest, repeating Anita's comment. 'Let's all get to sleep and carry on tomorrow.'

*

Everyone awoke the next morning to the sound of a loud gong reminiscent of the bell that summoned the kittendogs at meal times in the mansion house. This was followed by repeated knocking on the dormitory doors, followed by both Jet and Anita's voices.

'I have very good news; Mandy and Brutus have recovered from their ordeal and wish to meet you all as soon as possible after breakfast.'

Tonkas, being the most alert at that time in the morning, was the first to get out of bed and urged the others to do the same. By the time the others were fully awake he was fully dressed and out of the door, rushing as fast as he could to see his parents again. He made his way hurriedly to the infidel canteen, and standing at the serving hatch were Mandy and Brutus engrossed in conversation with Jet and Anita.

'You look a lot better than you did last night.'

'Oh we are,' replied Brutus. 'My powers could still be waning a little and we need to act fast before the king comes back after the conference.'

'Yes, I heard last night. We will be revived after we have eaten breakfast and we will be able to carry on where we left off before the woodlice were overcome,' answered Tonkas.

Breakfast was consumed with much relish by all the kittendogs, their appetite much increased with the activity of the previous day.

When the meal was over Mandy and Brutus gave an appreciative speech to thank all those involved with their rescue, not to mention the bravery involved. The matter of the dirty tricks department was raised, and also the question of destroying the remaining material before the return of the king.

Headeroonie Bill, yet again, was the first to make a suggestion.

'I think we should destroy anything in the Manipulations Laboratory, especially the dead woodlice, the food, and the tanks.

'We could steal all the fittings for our secret laboratory and that would leave this place empty except for the office.'

'Perhaps we could do one job at a time and not divide into groups as we did before. Start with

184

anything to do with the woodlice,' stated Mickel.

After the usual murmurings, this was agreed and the first course of action was to get rid of the woodlice remains, and so everyone set about their tasks.

Tonkas and Mickel were the first of the kittendogs to enter the evil laboratory and were greeted by the dreadful stench of decaying woodlice. Tonkas rushed over to the window and quickly opened them to get rid of the smell.

'We could get rid of this mess by throwing the woodlice remains out of the window, though we need a bucket or two to do the transfer.'

Luckily there were some in a cupboard under a sink, so they were immediately put to good use in order for this activity to be completed.

The next item on the agenda was to get rid of the evil-smelling liquid that served as food. Again the buckets were deployed, although this time the liquid was disposed of by pouring down the sink with copious amounts of water. This left the tanks and various other paraphernalia which were removed with the aid of trolleys, into the wash-up room adjacent to the infidel canteen. Thus, in a very quick time the last traces of anything associated with woodlice was removed from the laboratory.

Anita, who was so far absent from these proceedings, appeared on the scene wondering what the commotion was all about and was most surprised at the progress made so far in clearing the laboratory. She was unaware, however, of the woodlice remains that had been dispatched with haste from the windows. The most obvious thing to do would be to remove the evidence to the battle scene and then to burn them in the same way as the rest.

At this point Mickel spoke.

'We could get rid of the woodlice remains without the bother of conveying anything away. In that way we save time and effort.'

Anita agreed with this idea, realising that it was a very practical way of dealing with the problem.

'Just give me some tools, such as a hammer, and I can smash what is left of them and then hose the fluid away down the drains,' Mickel added.

Anita grabbed a toolbox from a bench and thrust it into Mickel's hands, beckoning to the door at the same time.

The pair left the laboratory and found their way to the outside, to the scene of destruction. Anita opened the toolbox as soon as it was convenient and a hammer was extracted. Handing the tool to Mickel, she said, 'Now here is your chance to exact more revenge on the enemy. Smash them into as many pieces as you can, the smaller the fragments the better, because the bits can be incorporated into the gravel driveway which leads to the porter's lodge. Make sure the bits are clean and then rake it all in well so no one notices anything.'

Mickel followed these orders with a great deal of enthusiasm, enjoying every minute of his relentless hammering on the woodlice shells, making them smaller and smaller with each action of his arm. Gradually fatigue set in and he was forced to stop. Getting up from his crouched position, he used his foot to finish the job and collect the pieces closer together.

'It would be easier to use a broom,' boomed Headeroonie Bill, suddenly appearing on the scene unannounced.

'Yes, I was about to get one,' answered Mickel, annoyed again at the tone of voice that was used. Mickel sauntered off to the workshops and surreptitiously acquired the necessary implements. Returning to the area of destruction, the task was completed far more effectively and the remnants temporarily found their way into a plastic dustbin.

This left the wet, slimy, glutinous mess remaining on the ground, some of which had adhered to Mickel's shoes. Again, the Training Academy workshop was visited and this time Mickel awarded himself with a length of hosepipe which he connected to an outside tap conveniently situated close to the scene of destruction. The mess was quickly washed away and the whole area was left cleaner than its initial condition, just leaving behind the dustbin of broken shell. Just as this was finished Anita showed up, timing her inspection so she did not have to do any of the work.

'Well done,' she exclaimed gratefully. 'You have done a wonderful job but now we need to get on with clearing out the Manipulations Laboratory.'

Mickel felt exhausted with all his exertions but nevertheless complied with this request and followed Anita back to the place he always considered to be one of the worst places he had ever seen, and did not look forward to the experience one little bit.

However, he was pleased to observe that anything to do with the giant killer woodlice had disappeared, and all that was left was the benching and stools. This was the next task, to remove all the laboratory fitments and move all the useful parts to the mansion house for the secret laboratory.

In order to commence the total annihilation of the king's empire, the bench tops were the first item to be tackled, their removal necessitating the removal of brackets from underneath. In order to accomplish this some of the cupboards had to be wheeled out of the way; this was easy since they were on wheels. Thus, the lengths of benching were dismantled and stacked on end; also the cupboards received a similar treatment. Luckily none of these activities interfered with the plumbing and electrical supplies, so all this work was quite easy. The laboratory therefore became an empty room with a few electrical cables and pipes which could be tidied at a future date. The benching and cupboards were then removed by the kittendogs, piece by piece, and taken out of the premises to the back yard. At a later date they were to be transported to the mansion house for use in the secret laboratory.

All that was left of the former laboratory was the office in the far corner which had remained untouched for some time. The precaution of returning every document, and everything else that had been removed back to its former location, now seemed unnecessary. The destruction of the king's empire was now almost complete. The giant killer woodlice were now gone as far as anyone knew, as was the place of their inception. It was now getting late to do much more, but there was still another thing to consider, and that was a visit to the second battle site to see what was left.

Headeroonie Bill gave the order to stop, and suggested that the few hours of daylight remaining would be better spent inspecting what remained of the encampment. To this end he asked for volunteers to accompany Anita and her van to pay another visit and to make sure the fires were now out. At once Mickel, Tonkas, and The Alisose immediately put up their hands and the working party was therefore decided.

Once more, Mickel left the laboratory for the outside back yard, this time accompanied by his colleagues for yet another task, although this time it surely would not be dangerous. The rest of the group assisted with the collection of shovels, sacks, and rakes, which would be required for the collection of ash material. Anita was of course the driver again, she being the only choice as no one else was available. However, this time there was no need for a surprise attack, and a shorter and easier route could be used to gain access to a different area of the encampment. The journey was uneventful, quite unlike the previous trip when stealth and care was a prerequisite. In a short time, the encampment was reached. Still expecting to see fires still burning, it came as a surprise to be greeted by piles of ashes and not even a trace of smoke.

'This makes our job easier,' said Anita. 'We do not have much to do other than shovel these ashes into the bags we have brought, and rake over what is left of the grass. Not many people come this way so hopefully no one will notice any difference. The grass will grow back eventually, but we need to collect everything together in the back of the van. Leave the shed behind because that looks as though it is original, but make sure everything else is gone.'

Mickel, Tonkas, and The Alisose set to work on this latest task, realising the importance of leaving everything just as it was, before the invasion of the giant killer woodlice. The king's empire was gradually being dismantled. All the woodlice had gone and also the laboratory in which they were probably conceived. Only the office was left and the man himself.

It required several trips of filled sacks of woodlice shell and ash, and also igloo parts, which looked somewhat similar to woodlice, only on a much larger scale. Most of the waste was in the form of ash. The heavy sacks required a lot of muscular activity to move, and care was needed in the transportation of the bags to the back of the van to prevent spillages.

Anita then made some comments regarding the disposal of the sacks of waste.

'We could empty the sacks on the floor of the workshop and sieve the ash, which can then be combined with the soil in our gardening department. The larger portions can be added to the rest of the woodlice shell that were crushed earlier by Mickel.'

This was the last comment Anita made before returning to the van to supervise the loading of the sacks. There was just enough room to accommodate all the bags of material in the back. She checked over the field where the woodlice had lived for an unknown period of time, and gave a final check of the shed where Mandy and Brutus had been held captive.

She then beckoned to the kittendogs to get in the van, and after they did so, she drove off.

The group were all very quiet during the journey back to the Training Academy with a sense of anti-climax. After the success of all the previous work there were seemingly fewer duties to be carried out, and the end of the quest was now in sight. There just remained the contents of the office to be sorted out, and how to deal with the king. He was bound to notice all the differences in his domain eventually and little could be done to effect any disguise. The battlefield would return to a natural state in time and the Manipulations Laboratory had all but disappeared. Perhaps this could be disguised as a seminar room or something similar to remove any semblance to a laboratory. In that way the king would lose all sense of direction. The only other way forward would be either to brainwash the king or somehow remove a portion of his memory.

All these thoughts were going through the kittendogs' minds as they journeyed on towards the Training Academy. These thoughts also applied to Anita, although she had to concentrate on her driving. However, the main consideration was to get back to the safety of the Training Academy at the end of another long and eventful day, and to consider all these points in the fresh light of a new day.

*

The kittendogs, the loyal Training Academy inventors, and Gregor, all had a very good night's sleep, comfortable in the knowledge that the giant killer woodlice would trouble them no more. Luck had been on their side so many times and now there was only one task left that required little effort, and that was to finish sorting through the king's office.

Anita then led the meeting once more after the usual breakfast.

'I think it is rather pointless sifting through all the contents of the office. We might as well clear everything out just as we did with the Manipulations Laboratory. We can then finish decorating the complex and make sure the whole lot is beyond recognition.'

Once more there followed a period of mumbling and murmuring, and finally Headeroonie Bill acted as spokesperson, agreeing with this idea and adding, 'I think if we all pull together we could get the job done that much quicker,' and then surprised everyone by marching towards the office and grasping the first thing he could get his hands on, this being the king's favourite armchair. Carrying it out back to the infidel canteen, he slammed it on the floor and pronounced, 'Well that's a start at least.'

Mickel then followed Headeroonie Bill back into the office and between them, they managed to manhandle the king's desk out its location and into the corridor. This was something of a miracle since the computer was still on it and survived its short journey without crashing to the floor. By now there was little left in the office, the heaviest object being a filing cabinet, which was moved out by using a trolley. Another trolley load completed the task, containing small electrical items and catering objects. All the items were left in the corridor during the redecorating of the laboratory in a different colour of paint in order to disguise its previous function. Unwanted electrical cables and plumbing were removed, the empty areas were filled with spare tables and chairs from the infidel canteen, and the job was finished.

These operations naturally took a great deal of time, in fact a whole day, and everyone involved was very tired by all the exertions. A quick meal was required and plenty of rest, completing yet another day.

*

The next morning it was decided to tackle the office equipment, and this would finish the job of getting rid of anything to do with the king's empire. This included the desk and computer and the rest of the objects left in the corridor the previous night. Instead of getting rid of these items by smashing them up, it was decided to make good use of them by incorporation into different areas of the Training Academy. Anita suggested that most of the office furniture go into her office and the associated paperwork could be sorted out at a more convenient time. By lunch time all this work had been completed and it was time for dining, but more importantly devising a strategy.

At this point Mandy and Brutus reunited themselves with everyone else, having fully recovered from their experience.

'Perhaps it is time to relinquish my spell on the king and the infidels,' said Brutus in a husky voice.

'Yes, perhaps it is,' replied Tonkas. 'Your spell has to stop sometime and it is making you rather weak. If they return we must hide away so we do not give anything away and just leave Anita, Jet, and Gregor behind. We had better get back to the mansion house and tidy ready for their return, otherwise the cook and maid might notice any changes.

'I am sure the spell is draining me of energy, though I suspect the woodlice creatures captured me to tap into my special powers, but I didn't let them succeed.'

'Good for you,' added Headeroonie Bill. 'Let's all go home and let our friends get back to their own lives, it must have been very disruptive for them to have us here all this time.'

'Yes, but don't forget I have frozen time still, almost, where the infidels are attending the conference, and they won't realise anything,' said Brutus. 'All will seem the same as they left it except for the laboratory. We had better go home. Some of us can go back in the barnmobile and the rest can walk. When we get back to the mansion and offload The Alisose we can then drive back for the others. When we are settled in, Brutus can let go of his spell and in the meantime Anita, Jet, and Gregor can remove evidence of our stay. I will need time to concentrate on the spell.'

The conversation then closed, with everyone departing for possibly for the last time. Tonkas was feeling sad and so was Anita as she said, 'We must make arrangements to meet again soon. Look for smoke from our incinerator as a signal that all is safe for you to visit.'

That was the last time she spoke as the barnmobile filled with kittendogs to capacity, with the rest walking behind. Mandy and Brutus sat in the back, making sure they could see Anita and her colleagues until they disappeared out of sight. The Alisose drove the barnmobile to the back door of the mansion house and they all got out, climbing the stairs to the bedrooms which were just as they left them, except for a musty smell. The latter was dispelled by opening the windows of all the rooms, before the group relocated to the kitchen to check over the condition.

The Alisose remembered that she had to go back and collect more kittendogs still making their way on foot, and so left the building on her own. The barnmobile started immediately, with the turn of the key exhibiting its reliability once more. The journey was more boring without any company but that was compensated by the reduction in duration as the group was soon reached. This group included Mandy and Brutus, who made good use of the time by relating some of their experiences to a captivated audience.

The next trip was to include Sylvate and Mickel and nearly everyone else except for Mareekoid, who wanted to make her own way, preferring her own company as usual. The Alisose drove away once more, Mareekoid stating that she wished to be alone and there was no need for another trip, as she would walk all the way back on her own. The Alisose reluctantly agreed, relieved that another trip was not required, and she would have more time to adjust to life back at the mansion. There would also more be more time to spend with Mandy and Brutus in the future. With that thought in mind she drove away. This time the journey seemed a lot shorter but also boring, since no one wished to engage in conversation. Perhaps all the previous activities had exhausted them. Darkness was closing in as the back door of the mansion was reached and the passengers tumbled out, not caring where they were.

'Such is this sense of anti-climax,' stated Mickel finally. 'I have nothing left to destroy,' he moaned.

'Never mind, I am sure that there is something for you to do that is more constructive, like the secret laboratory, for example. When that is finished we can go back to inventing things, just like the old days,' said Sylvate.

Rumblings of discontent were still going on as the back door of the mansion was reached, and the gathering found their way upstairs to the dormitories for further cleaning and tidying.

There was a noise from the back door just as the dormitories were gained as Mareekoid arrived, gasping for breath, as she had run all the way back.

Brutus was the next to make an appearance and stated, 'I have given up my spell over the infidels and the king. Soon they will be returning, but there will be no time lag as far as they are concerned. They will think that they have just returned from their conference.'

CHAPTER 13

The Demise of the King

The kittendogs started to settle down to life at the mansion in a much happier state of mind, now that Mandy and Brutus were back with them. It was even better that they assumed their previous control over their offspring. There was also much relief that the cook and maid were gone, at least for the time being. On the other hand, this was tempered by the fact that Mandy and Brutus were still under par and required a great deal of cooperation and understanding to cope with the basic requirements of running the household. This was not such an onerous task as it seemed as the kittendogs were now well used to tending for themselves for some time. It was true that Anita, Jet, and Gregor held much supervision over the juniors but the kittendogs were by now much more independent than before. The worries and concerns of the occupants of the mansion house were far less considerable than those of the Training Academy.

At the same time Anita and her friends were far more fully occupied restoring the infidel canteen, the sleeping arrangements, and most of all the laboratories to the same condition prior to the conference. The Manipulations Laboratory was the area that showed the most change; it was hoped that the king would not notice that the area which had witnessed his evil ways were now gone forever. It was now getting late and it was assumed that the king and his followers would not return until the morning, so the best thing to do was to get as much sleep and recuperation as possible.

*

Anita was wakened by the sound of a motorcar engine revving in the back entrance car park. This was followed by the sound of loud voices that Anita recognised as belonging to some of the inventors. Getting out of her bed and peering through a gap in the curtains confirmed that this was the case. The best course of action was to rouse Jet and Gregor and put her plan into operation. This was to greet the arrivals, but at all costs keep them away from the king's laboratory, and anything else to do with him. There was no time to waste; Jet and Gregor received a quick shake, and making sure they were awake, Anita rushed down the stairs ready to greet the first of the entourage. Opening the door, Anita observed that the inventors were already getting out of the vehicle and staggering in her direction, apparently the worse for wear. Anita could smell alcohol on their breath as one of them attempted to speak, and she desired to deny them access.

Just at that moment another vehicle arrived and to her dismay the king got out from the rear door, accompanied by the cook and maid, holding what appeared to be awards and certificates.

'Sorry about my colleagues' condition,' explained the king. 'They got a bit carried away with the celebrities last night and have not yet recovered. They can stay outside in the fresh air for the time being and hopefully can recover their composure. In the meantime, I would like to unload our belongings.'

Anita observed a softening in his voice from what she had become accustomed to in the years she had known him. The tall, gaunt figure of the king with his balding pate sauntered to the rear of the limousine, and opening the boot, extracted a number of suitcases having previously relieved himself of some baggage to his subordinates. However, he grimly held on to his most prized possession, a brown clipboard attached to which was a pencil on a long length of string, used to record thoughts that went through his mind.

Anita thought that both the cook and maid had improved in their demeanour, having encountered them in her previous visits to the mansion house.

It was then the king spoke for the first time since he left for the awards conference and ceremony. 'If you don't mind we would like to freshen up before we start the day's work. Please take these trifles to my office,' pointing towards the suitcases and other items. 'We must drive to our accommodation block and see you later in the day.'

Anita's first thoughts were of dread and horror, as it was obvious that the king had not forgotten about his office and presumably his laboratory as well. The spell that Brutus had imposed on him had not erased his memory on this matter so something drastic had to be done. It came as some relief that at least the king would be out of the way for a little time, but this could only serve to delay the inevitable. Another plan had to be devised and the sooner this was done the better it would be.

Finally, Jet and Gregor arrived just as the vehicles drove away.

'What can we do to help?'

'We need something to scan the king when he makes his next appearance, to see if we can alter his memory. We could use all these surveillance cameras around the Training Academy and watch his every movement,' suggested Anita.

The three of them then set about checking all the cameras to ensure they were all working properly, and also making the correct connections into the security room just as they did when the invasion took place. This time an infrared beam and alarm was incorporated into each camera to detect any inconsistences with the person the camera detected. All anyone could do now was to wait for the unwanted arrival of the king.

To keep them occupied Anita and the others brought some paperwork from the king's office to check over. At all times someone was present in the security room keeping a close watch on the camera monitors. Amongst all the papers were manuscripts for a series of books appertaining to management written by the king, but not yet published. Volume one had the title "How to Create Problems", volume two was called "How to Solve Problems" and the third volume was entitled "How to Get the Credit for Solving Problems". There was also a series of files for all the staff involved in the Training Academy, with special reference on how to exploit their weak points, and a section on how to disregard their strengths. There were very many files to go through but the sense of reward in finding out about the king's activities was rudely interrupted by the sound of a buzzer. The king had arrived in the laboratory complex!

A state of panic immediately followed amongst the members of the group, with nobody knowing what to do for the best. There was only thing for it and that was to congregate around the monitors and to observe what would happen. Luckily the cameras were set on record so any happenings could be documented for all time.

The king entered the outside corridor, apparently looking for his laboratory and trying the handles to gain entry. Unfortunately for him he was unsuccessful. A strange thing then happened to him. A red beam from one of the security cameras came into contact with the centre of his back and he started to stagger around uncontrollably. A hole was the result of the red beam, which was becoming larger and emitting a substance which dripped on the floor, smelling of molten wax. Within the hole there was evidence of electrical wiring and components which were giving off smoke and sparks. With a few more steps the king came to a stop and then crashed unceremoniously to the floor on his face. After a few twitches of his arms and legs the king finally stopped moving, and the sparks also ceased at the same time. The king appeared to have expired!

Sarcastically, the small group of characters assembled in the security room gave a whoop of delight and Anita was the first to rush into the corridor to the aid of the king. Her attempts at revival were to no avail and she pronounced him non-extant to Gregor and Jet as they approached the remains. Anita was the first to summon enough courage to reach inside the gaping hole in the king's back and withdrew a handful of tangled wires. Pulling at the wires, a gentle tug was sufficient enough to release a printed circuit board containing electronic chips and processors. There were spaces in the circuit board where there should have been other microprocessors, although there were only two which were clearly labelled. One was labelled sense of humour and the other compassion and humanity.

Anita drew her own conclusions from this.

'I always knew he was a serious and cold-hearted, unfeeling individual, incapable of showing any consideration to the inventors in the Training Academy. Help me get his remains onto an operating trolley in my laboratory and I will drive around to the mansion and inform the kittendogs.'

Jet and Gregor assembled two trolleys and tied them together with the king's belt and tie. Using the trolleys as a makeshift stretcher on wheels, the remains were transported into Anita's laboratory and any leftover parts were moved in the same manner.

'I always thought the king was some sort of robot,' noted Jet. 'His actions were stereotyped and callous, and his departure will not be missed by the great majority of staff. I wonder if Anita would mind if we started to dismantle this collection of electro-mechanical paraphernalia that went under the guise of a decent human being.'

'I don't see why not.'

'Right, let's get started then.'

The assembly was manhandled into the laboratory and unceremoniously dumped on an empty length of bench. The pair of them wasted no time in applying screwdrivers, spanners, and any other tool that was suitable for the operation of mechanical dissection. The limbs and head were removed with ease, leaving the torso which was turned over, revealing the vast hole in the back. The hole was so large that it was very easy to see right through the body to the other side of the laboratory.

'I see there is no heart, just a mechanical pump,' observed Jet.

'That's no surprise to me,' was the reply.

Before any other actions could be undertaken there was a crash on the door as Anita rushed in, followed by the kittendogs, led by Mickel who commented, 'I wish I had the chance of bestowing all this destruction. It would have been a fitting end to all that I dislike about the treatment that has been meted out to me in recent weeks. I would like all this rubbish to be incinerated to the point of utter oblivion.'

Everyone else present nodded in agreement and stood to one side as Mickel set about salvaging what could be used elsewhere in the form of electrical and mechanical components. The rest of the parts were dumped into a large wheeled bin ready to be dealt with at a future time. Brutus gave a big cheer and announced that he would arrange for a party to be held in the Training Academy grounds. His favourite musical bands were to be invited, called "The Rolling Bones" and "Belton Ron", and because they were locally based the concert of all concerts was going to happen the very next day.

The group stared in amazement at each other and at Brutus in particular.

'There is hardly any time to get things ready,' they all said in unison.

'Don't worry; I have summoned all the staff of the Training Academy to attend, even including the infidels. Things will never be the same after this,' answered Brutus.

As if by magic, throngs of people arrived without prior warning, in a miscellany of transport. Some of the vehicles were loaded to capacity containing supplies of food, drink, picnic furniture, and musical equipment, and most important of all, a large marquee. There was no shortage of volunteers to erect all the equipment in readiness for the great event, and word quickly spread around the neighbourhood, resulting in even more volunteers.

All this was a result of the mystical powers of Brutus, who exercised his natural ability to great effect, achieving the impossible in a very short period of time. The kittendogs were astounded with such a great amount of work without much involvement on their part, and retired for the night at ease with themselves and looking forward to a new day.

*

The next day arrived soon enough. The kittendogs slept through a spell of intense activity, all the work they normally would have done completed by the task force from nowhere and everywhere. The party went on all day, not finishing until late at night, leaving everyone involved thoroughly exhausted. The kittendogs made many new friends in that time, many of whom were past and present students and staff of the Training Academy. The event attracted the staff back to the Training Academy, having found out about the king's unfortunate end. Anita and Jet were very pleased since they had struggled for a long period of time trying to maintain the level of service expected of them. Many of the loyal staff had deserted their posts in the past, having given up working under the king's rule of oppression.

Late in the day Anita made a confession to the kittendogs when clearing up in the kitchen. It was she who actually arranged the so-called invasion by Umphadee and Umphadah. She knew that these two strange forest dwellers were great friends of the kittendogs, and thought their input could be of importance in the quest of finding Mandy and Brutus. She also arranged that the pair of them would put the key to the Manipulations Laboratory on to her bunch of keys, having pretended to lose them. It was also Umphadee and Umphadah who arranged the clues in the hollow rocks and locating the large boulder. This chain of events explained her strange behaviour at times, she said.

'Well the end justifies the means,' stated Brutus. He attempted to say more but the sound of Belton Ron playing "Hatchett Man" stopped him in his tracks. This was his favourite song and also appealed to the inventors in the Training Academy. Any conversation was drowned out by the loud volume of the music as the group which had congregated around the group grew larger and larger.

This proved to be the climax of the concert and although more songs were played they did not have the same impact on the throng of people. Many of them drifted away when the smell of food pervaded the air. The finale of the party was the firework display, which commenced as the daylight began to fade.

However, the mingling of kittendogs and inventors continued well into the night and many new friendships were forged that night, which were to last for a long time into the future. One result was that the inventors and kittendogs decided to corroborate their investigations into the manufacture and distribution of gadgets to the benefit of all mankind. The secret laboratory was to be completed in the near future with help from the inventors, and there was to be no more need for secrecy.

All this, however, was to happen at a later date as further discussion was hampered by the arrival by the cook and maid on the scene, carrying food on trays. This action was greeted with surprise by the kittendogs, having been all too familiar with their behaviour in the past. It seemed that a complete transformation had come over them and both the cook and maid were to cease being enemies. The last vestige of the king's dominance was over for good.

As the fireworks reached their finale the kittendogs gathered together and Brutus started a speech, thanking all concerned for his rescue along with Mandy's at the same time. The entire group held their hands together with Tonkas in the centre. A strange event then took place when they circled around Tonkas and then started to chant:

Barnpotting across the Luniverse in a barnmobile and with Thomas Pigglewick.

Barnpotting across the Luniverse, always going backwards never in reverse.

This was repeated over and over again as the group continued to circle around the unfortunate Tonkas, until a white cloud descended upon them, forming a funnel-like appearance. The pointed end of this structure then sucked Tonkas off his feet and in a spinning motion he ascended higher and higher until he was gone!

CHAPTER 14

Back to the Present

Thomas awoke in a railway carriage and became somewhat shaken as the train came to an abrupt halt. He rubbed his eyes and looked around. There was only one other person in the carriage, and that was his father huddled in the far corner next to the window. His head was bowed but he was moving it very slightly in an up-and-down fashion, as though he was neither asleep nor fully awake. Thomas decided to settle the matter, and rising from his own seat, he shuffled the few steps required to reach him and tapped him on the shoulder.

'Hurry up, we have reached our destination. Let's get out and explore this place before we go back again. It would be boring just to stay in the train and not get out. We can always get another one back.'

Michael, his father, finally came to his senses and continued to nod his head, but this time in agreement.

'Good idea, I was just nodding off to sleep, I think some fresh air would do me good.'

The two of them alighted from the carriage, closing the door behind them, and made their way to the rear of the train to the exit of the station. Just as they approached the last carriage, a figure got out holding green and red flags. Thomas walked closer to him and gave a gasp. Thinking to himself, he uttered, 'I seem to recognise this person, as though I have seen him before somewhere,' and without Michael observing what was going on, the man slipped a sealed envelope into Thomas's pocket.

This is rather strange, thought Thomas. He decided it would be wise not to open the letter straight away but to find a quiet time and place to carry out this action. Therefore, he followed close behind his father, towards the exit of the station, and hid the envelope in his pocket after folding it in half. He noticed that his father was carrying a picnic hamper and so deduced that they would be eating their lunch outdoors.

Coincidentally, his father spoke for the second time, the pair having exchanged only a few words so far on this trip.

'I have devised an excursion I hope you will be satisfied with. We will walk along a path that parallels the railway line until we come across the next station, where we will catch another train. On the way we will stop at a park and have our lunch and perhaps you can play with the facilities which are provided.'

'Very good,' replied Thomas, and he saw this as a chance to open the letter and read its contents in secret, if Michael could be distracted in some way. The path seemed familiar to him and even more so when it opened out into a field enclosed by a stone wall. In the field were many areas of burnt grass and scorched earth, with a hut at the far end. *I seem to have been here before*, he thought.

Michael decided to have lunch, using the low wall as a seat, although Thomas protested as there was nothing to interest him.

'Where are the facilities that you promised?'

'I must have been mistaken, or else they have been removed judging by the burnt patches in the grass. It is past our normal lunch time so we might as well eat now.'

Thomas shrugged his shoulders and did not reply, wishing he had the chance to open the letter without being seen, and had to eat the sandwiches and extras without displaying his frustration. The last course of the meal was the drinks, consumed with haste as it was beginning to rain.

'Let's shelter in that hut,' exclaimed Michael. 'We should find some shelter in case the rain gets any harder.'

The pair made a dash for the hut as the rain became more incessant. Thomas was the first to reach the door, and using his shoulder he charged it open. Having nothing to carry and being the youngest, he covered the distance much faster than his father. He had hoped he would gain enough time to open the door and read the letter but he was foiled once again as Michael soon followed him inside the shed.

After his eyes became accustomed to the dim light Thomas had the impression of having been in this shed before, or at least somewhere resembling it. Michael noticed that Thomas was becoming pale and suggested he sat down and rest for a while.

'I don't like this place; it makes me feel sick.'

'We will have to wait until the rain stops and then we can go.'

Thomas gave the surroundings a detailed inspection and only grew to dislike the interior even more. There was slime all over the floor and some old rope and chairs, as though someone had been held captive. The rain was making an incessant clattering on the corrugated roof, annoying Thomas even more. Michael sensed his son's aggravation and suggested that they leave the dark and depressing place and make a run to the nearest shelter. Thomas concluded this action was the lesser of two evils and wasted no time in making for the door. Tugging at his father's arm, he urged him to find shelter under the nearest tree, running over an area of broken pieces of shell mixed with a great deal of ash material. His father was perplexed at this debris but Thomas was becoming more aware that something sinister had happened here and not so long ago, otherwise grass would have grown over the area. The shelter of the tree placated him as he was pleased at making an escape from the shed, and became even better humoured when the rain eased to be replaced by sunshine.

'I think it is a good time to leave and get back to

the station where I left the car,' suggested Michael. 'We need to continue on the footpath which is alongside the railway until we reach the lower terminus.'

Thomas followed his father out of the field, finding an area where the wall had been broken down to ground level, making it easier to surmount. There was a line of flattened grass through another field, at the far end of which was a line of trees. There appeared to be an entrance to another path at the treeline but this was too far away to be certain, so the only way to find out was to trek across the field.

'There must be a reason why the grass across the field had been trampled flat,' Michael explained.

Thomas and his father made their way towards the line of trees, not speaking to each other for quite some time and getting their feet wet in the process. It came as a relief to Thomas to reach the tree and luckily there was a path after all.

'I am very glad to leave that field behind. I think something dreadful might have happened here, and the shed was awful,' moaned Thomas.

'Oh do stop complaining, this is supposed to be a pleasant day out. I thought a train ride and then a walk would please you.'

'It's that field and hut. As soon as we put some distance between that area and ourselves, the better I will feel. Besides, we need to do something else than ride on trains and then walk back to where we started.'

'Well there is a shop at the other end and it sells the sort of books you like to read,' said Michael.

This pleased Thomas and he felt much better with this idea. By now the sun was shining, the sky was entirely blue without a cloud in the sky, and things were improving by the minute as far as Thomas was concerned. The two of them chatted happily to pass the time, playing "I Spy" along the way, coming across many cyclists and other walkers, curiously all travelling in the opposite direction as though they were all travelling with some purpose in mind. A river appeared to the right of them with children playing on a small beach using pieces of wood as makeshift boats. To the left, a line of railway track emerged from a tunnel, and before long a train with two carriages steamed past them. Both driver and fireman waved before the train disappeared from sight. Thomas had a suspicion that he had seen both of these characters in a different time and place and to confuse him even more, the person who gave him the letter earlier in the day also waved from the guard's compartment!

The walk continued and still the pair did not engage in conversation, although Thomas noticed some birds that looked somewhat artificial in that the feathers did not seem real, nor did anything else about them. When they flew from the branches on which they were perching, their wings gave a clanking sound, making the birds even more artificial. By now the footpath paralleled the railway, separated from it only by a fence and slightly raised embankment. A signal appeared into view, indicating that the station was getting closer. Around the next bend in the footpath the train that passed them earlier was stationary and letting off a little steam while it was awaiting clearance to gain access to the station itself.

The pair even walked past the train, Thomas observing that there were not many passengers in the carriages. The guard seemed to be missing, but the driver and fireman stood still in the cab.

Michael then spoke for the first time in quite a while, indicating the station was now very close and informing Thomas that the bookshop would be open and they would hopefully be partaking of some refreshments. They carried on walking until the path widened, and then emerged onto a tarmacked road. To the left another path veered away from them, which led to the station building and platform. Opening an iron gate which allowed entrance to the station, the pair made for the shop which was a simple lean-to construction adjoining the main building. Above the door was inscribed the shopkeeper's name, this being Walter Mitty. Daring to go in, he was rewarded with the sight of books written by his favourite author, but on observing the person behind the counter, he became somewhat perplexed. Thomas was sure he had seen this character before, just like the guard on the train.

'Good grief, you look somewhat pale,' commented Michael. 'Are you alright?' he added.

'Of course,' was the reply, 'I am so excited at seeing all these books for sale in one place, they are difficult to find in this sort of quantity.'

Michael decided to purchase just two of the books, stating that they could return one day and buy some more. Thomas then spotted some volumes of "The Good Management Guide" but could not decipher the author. Again, Thomas thought that he seen this before but could not remember where and when. In the meantime, it was time to go home as he had to go to work the next day. Having completed the transaction, the pair left the shop and made for the station exit the way that they had come. Just before they left the station Thomas and Michael walked past the engine driver and fireman, and Thomas had an uncomfortable feeling he had met them before, just like all the other staff of this strange preserved railway. Thomas felt rather relieved to be going home after what appeared to him to be a curious afternoon to say the least.

Father and son left the railway the same way they had come earlier in the day. Unwittingly Thomas put his hand in the pocket that did not contain the letter and pulled out a packet he did not even realise was there. Managing to conceal the packet from Michael, he looked at the label which read "Transportation Gravel" and "Use Carefully". Thomas was taken aback by this as it resembled modeller's railway ballast that was used on his model railway back home. Furthermore, Thomas was perplexed by the description written on the packet, as he always thought this was perfectly safe to use. Hurriedly, he replaced the item back into his pocket, unseen by his father's prying eyes. Soon the pair reached the car park, Michael handed his son a bag containing the books that were recently purchased.

'Perhaps you would like to have a look at these books while I drive home. This would give you something to do on the way back.'

Thomas gracefully accepted the present and said nothing for the rest of the trip. He became totally engrossed in the books, not even showing the remotest interest in the view from the window of the car. The journey was relatively short and the roads free of heavy traffic, so the trip was over for the day as Michael parked the car outside the family home.

The evening followed the usual boring pattern of watching television after the evening meal, washing dishes, and preparing sandwiches for the following day's work and school. Thomas was free to pursue his favourite hobbies of working and playing on his computer with any other free time reading one of his many books, all pursued in the family office located in the loft of the home. He was luckier than most of his peers at school in that he was not required to partake of any domestic chores so all his time was used in pursuing anything he wanted. Time passed quickly as usual in the household, and soon it was time for Thomas to go bed.

Undressing for the night, Thomas noticed that he still had the transportation granules and the unopened letter in his trouser pocket. Now that the rest of the family had retired for the night, now was the ideal opportunity to open the letter and find out what it was all about. It was still sealed and in a rather crumpled condition, but Thomas thought it was about time to read it.

The letter was carefully typed and on the first page it stated that it was from Headeroonie Bill, leader of the Preservationists, and Anita Moontogs, Technical Lead of the Training Academy Inventors. It read:

We, the undersigned, would like to take this opportunity to thank Thomas Pigglewick for the role he played in the return of

Mandy and Brutus to the kittendog fraternity. He was summoned by the magical powers bestowed upon Brutus by the supernatural being known as Mana. By Thomas's own special powers a greater threat was revealed in the form of the king, affecting the very existence of the inhabitants of both the Great Mansion and the Training Academy itself. Without Thomas's input the quest would never have been completed.

With the demise of the king there will be a better sense of camaraderie between the Training Academy and its inventors now that the effect of his interfering ways has been removed. We may contact Thomas in the future if we need any further assistance with any future problems we may have.

As a final comment we have realised that negotiations at an early stage are far superior to one person's idea that is relentlessly pursued without any thought and consideration of the consequences it may have on the individuals concerned. To that end, we have reduced the powers of any leader so he has to consult a committee at every stage and any action is only taken when a majority vote is reached.

After reading the last sentence, Thomas drifted off to sleep.